THIRST

THIRST

THE DESERT TRILOGY
SHULAMITH HAREVEN

TRANSLATED
BY HILLEL HALKIN
WITH THE AUTHOR

MERCURY HOUSE ✒ SAN FRANCISCO

Published in the United States by Mercury House, San Francisco, California,
a nonprofit publishing company devoted to the free exchange of ideas and guided
by a dedication to literary values. Visit us at http://www.mercuryhouse.org.

UNITED STATES CONSTITUTION, FIRST AMENDMENT:
Congress shall make no law respecting an establishment of religion, or
prohibiting the free exercise thereof; or abridging the freedom of speech,
or of the press; or the right of the people peaceably to assemble,
and to petition the Government for a redress of grievances.

Mercury House and colophon are registered trademarks
of Mercury House, Incorporated.

cover, interior design, typesetting: Thomas Christensen
editing/production: Thomas Christensen, Carol
Christensen, Kirsten Janene-Nelson, Sarah Rosenthal

Manufactured in the United States of America

Library of Congress Cataloging-in-Publication Data:
Hareven, Shulamith
[Novels. English. Selections]
Thirst : the desert trilogy / Shulamith Hareven ;
translated by Hillel Halkin with the author.
p. cm.
Contents: The miracle hater—Prophet—After childhood.
ISBN 1-56279-088-9 (pbk. : alk. paper)
1. Hareven, Shulamith—Translations into English.
I. Halkin, Hillel, 1939– .
II. Hareven, Shulamith. Sone ha-nisim. English.
III. Hareven, Shulamith. Navi. English.
IV. Hareven, Shulamith. Ahara ha-yaldut. English.
V. Title.

892.4'36—dc20   96-5152
CIP

FIRST EDITION
9 8 7 6 5 4 3 2 1

CONTENTS

THE MIRACLE HATER

—

3

PROPHET

—

63

AFTER CHILDHOOD

—

129

THIRST

THE
MIRACLE
HATER

They kept leaving all the time. One from a town, two from a family, they fled the settled districts of the land of Egypt to join those who had left before them. They did not go far: no further than the nearest oasis or the first gully that had a spring. They sought only to put the sand between themselves and Egypt, to get away from its lords and officials. No more than that.

They had no leaders. Perhaps no customs either. They dwelt in their oases, where they led lives of lowly, grinding, sunbaked poverty, shuffling about in black rags, whistling to their flocks that were as black and gaunt as they, often subsisting by robbery. Now and then troops were sent out to restore order; yet this did not happen often, for such expeditions were known to be perilous. The barefoot oases-dwellers could deal the soldiers a quick, sharp blow and melt off into the sands where even the wind lost all track of them. Year after year the corpses left by both sides were scorched by the sun until they could no longer be told apart from the bones of the earth itself. Every bit of yarn or iron had been stripped from them long ago.

Occasionally, half stealth and half insolence, known by his black rags, by the deep, grimy bronze of his tough, saurian hide, and by the furtive way he moved, one of the fugitives would approach the adobe wall of a farm. His shadow flitted over it like a raven's; whoever sensed it, remarked: There goes one of them. Then, a teal snatched from a canal or a watermelon in season wrapped in the folds of his cloak, he bounded quickly back into the desert, leaving behind him a mocking flurry of oaths. The farm workers drove him off lackadaisically, staring at his brazen flight with a stolid, passive amazement.

People held them in low repute. Vagabonds, they were called contemptuously, castaways. Not even the poorest slave, not even the meanest day laborer, would give his daughter in marriage to anyone belonging to this outcast band of Hebrews. In fact, though, little was seen of them. Those who left had left for good. The sand ruled them off utterly from the denizens of the watered farmland with its canals and ditches, its seasons and crop cycles, its masters and slaves, its borders and hedges, its settled ways that revolved as slowly each day as the water buffalo turns around the waterwheel.

Sanded in, bound to no man, they waited.

There were others too. Long settled in one place, they had become like Egyptians. At any time one of their boys might be spied perched high in a date grove on a ladder propped against a palm frond, harvesting the clusters of fruit with a short knife, or draping their heavy, pendulous abundance with a net against the multitude of birds, or simply staring down at the crossroads below while playing away on a flute. They belonged to the house of Tsuri, mastersingers and musicians without peer who worked for the wealthy families of Raamses and lived in spacious homes in the shade of the date palms. Walking out at dusk to the nearby canal, they stood bathed in a great, golden radiance, in the honeyed, leonine light pouring over the plain, fishing with the Egyptian boys, sometimes with hooks and nets from the bank and sometimes from their high-sparred boats. Barefoot and wet, dripping light and sparkles of water, they brought their catch home in panniers full of quivering, silvery, sinewy fish, their voices mingling with the calls of the gorgeous birds that fished at this hour too. Wherever man made way, hordes of pelicans, pink flamingos, white egrets, and ibises descended with a great flap of wings and no end of commotion.

This hour of Egypt's grace was never missed by the lady Ashlil, a Hebrew woman who was the widow of a local official. Stepping out on her rooftop thatched with palm fronds, she peeled the fruit handed her by one of her young male attendants and leisurely watched the light slowly dropping like dark honey over the ambering, the silvering, the darkling water. Many years before, while still an unbetrothed girl, she had seen, at precisely this time of day, a leopard with man's eyes standing by the old canal that had since fallen into disuse. Now, every evening, her keen eyes were trained on that spot. But there were no leopards, only the white egrets that followed the water buffaloes, and the Hebrew hands shouldering their burdens and singing their hushed songs in which there was not a shred of hope. The Hebrews had multiplied greatly and not all of them could find work in and around Raamses. They descended on the province, innumerable flocks of men and women who stood long hours in the sun, or sat in the shade of the baked-brick walls, looking for work. The Egyptians would come, take the five or ten of them that they needed, and drive the rest off. For a while they would vanish; yet soon they were back again, mute in the fly-ridden sunlight, waiting. Even when the busy season was over in the fields they went on waiting, more of them every year. There was no getting rid of them. In the end they were forbidden to bear children. It was time they squatted elsewhere. It was time they went away. But the Hebrews did not go. Their wives cunningly gave birth in secret lairs and were back at work a few hours later. Often they could not retrieve the newborn child from its hiding place. Wild animals sniffed out the lairs.

On the feast of Osiris, when, in an ark made of bulrushes,

each Egyptian household floated a painted, decorated little image of the god upon the Nile and its great canals, the wives of the Hebrew laborers cunningly floated their infants on the water too. Sometimes these arks came to rest in the tall, silent reeds; sometimes the foundlings were rescued by Egyptian families, who took them to be the annual reincarnation of the god Osiris himself. This was nothing to wonder at: everybody knew that life and death belonged to the Nile, that most supreme, that mightiest of rivers whose vast waters were the water of life. Even barren women whose wombs had turned to wood and stone were known to have conceived through them. Sometimes it was enough to suck on the rushes in the thick growth by the riverside in order to become pregnant. Where, if not from the same slime, did all those millions of frogs, all that ceaseless fecundity, come from?

Baita was nearly five years old when the hired hand Milka gave birth to Eshkhar, in total darkness, in a hidden burrow at the far end of the Hebrews' camp. She had stumbled down there during the day and now stood frightened in one corner, a thumb in her mouth, listening to the unseen squatting woman laboring to deliver her child. At first Baita thought that she had descended to this place in order to empty her bowels. The burrow was hot, cramped, and full of grunts, like the presence of a host of furry beasts. Milka paid no attention to Baita, who, watching from where she crouched in the corner, strove to make out the dim shapes, to decipher the darkness and the heat.

Then, as if the furry animals had gone, it was over. The burrow became empty and clean. A gust of wind, a thirsty night breeze, blew down into it; the clouds broke away from the moon and a whitish light shone inside. Milka rose groaning. She wiped herself and her baby and carried it to the entrance of the burrow. A boy, she grunted to herself. A boy.

She tied his cord with a piece of string and, taking a date

from her clothing, chewed it carefully and smeared its pulp with her thumb on his palate. He whimpered a bit and fell still.

Then she saw Baita, eyes gleaming in the corner. Wearily she asked if she had been there all the time. Baita nodded.

For a long while Milka said nothing. Then, digging a hole with a peg she had brought, she thoughtfully buried the after-birth and the other remains. Finally, with a quick motion, she placed the naked, shivering child in Baita's arms.

—Take him home with you. His name is Eshkhar.

Baita clutched the boy and ran with him to her father's hut. Though the women there sought to take him from her, she re-fused to part with him. It was all they could do to persuade her to let them change her soaked clothes. The child was as much her own as if she had borne him herself. She laid him down close to her and did not fall asleep until morning came with the scrabble of chickens among the thatched shacks, the creaky rounds of the buffalo tied to its wheel, the thump-and-stomp of the cattle being taken out to pasture, the splash of fresh milk into jugs, all the clamor and commotion of watering troughs. Eshkhar slept at her side.

Sometimes it was Milka who nursed him, always hurriedly between chores; sometimes one of the women from the house of her father Yitzhar, anyone who happened to have milk in her breasts. Sometimes Baita herself dripped fatty yellow buffalo milk into his mouth. He'll be sick, they warned her. But Eshkhar grew and thrived. Eventually they strapped him to her back, so that, when dusk dropped, one might have thought that a strange, humped little animal was roaming the village and bleat-ing from its hump. One tuft of Baita's hair was always wet from being sucked by the child. Always the same one.

They grew up as one body.

A year or so later, Milka, who now went to work each day in an Egyptian house, was large with child again. She had been admonished not to take chances, but, apart from binding her stomach to keep it well in, made light of the advice. There's no harm in them, she said. The Egyptian maids were all her friends, and besides, if she did not go to work, who would feed all those hungry children whose father could be counted on for nothing? Yet her time came sooner than she had calculated and found her shaking out her mistress's rugs. She sought to slip off to the fields, but was seen by a little servant who ran to tell the lady of the house. The lady was in mourning that week for a son who had died, and could not bear the thought of a Hebrew giving birth when she herself was bereaved. What can explain this dreadful fertility of the Hebrews, she was wont to lament to her husband, except their working in the mud of the Nile, which everyone knows is good for childbearing? Just look how they've settled down to spawn here with the frogs, flies, and lice; will you tell me when we ever had so many frogs and flies before? We go around scratching as though with the mange because of their filth. They've taken all the blessing from our lives. This plaint was spoken in a hoarse, throaty tone and accompanied by the melancholy, slow, unceasing tinkle of her anklets.

Now, when her little maidservant came to tell her that the Hebrew woman was in labor, she jumped to her feet and an evil thought came out of her like a spark. She summoned the Canaanite overseer, an evil-hearted man. A great hush settled over the house and all its frightened occupants. The Canaanite seized Milka, tied her by the feet, and hung her head-down from the nearest tree. All day long her swollen belly heaved horribly like a dying fish, making the tree, the village, the earth itself shudder. Then it stopped.

When night came, several of the Hebrew men set out. They knew they would not catch the Canaanite. But they did waylay a wagon of Egyptians. It was the feast of the firstborn, and the

Egyptians were off to celebrate in a painted cart decorated with bulrushes and feathers. Most of them were tipsy. They never heard the lurking fury ahead. They had no foreboding of it. The Hebrews murdered them quickly, every one of them, eldest sons all, from the age of five to twenty. In silence they worked, panting with fear, in a cold sweat; then fled. Hurry, hurry, they urged their wives, we cannot even stay until the morning. They took what they could and quickly made for the sands.

Afterwards they waited for the punitive expedition. It never came. Still, the fear remained and they kept moving further away, until even the pointed tips of Egypt's scattered pyramids could no longer be seen on the horizon. There was nothing but sand. On the fifth day they found the camp of the castaways, those who had left the settled land long before them and pitched their tents nearby. At first they spoke to them haughtily: *they* would yet return to Egypt, they were just waiting for things to blow over, for the old pharaoh to die. But the castaways laughed in their faces. You can never go back, they said, never. You might as well get used to it now.

They waited. Gradually they too built booths and mud huts in their new abode. And went on waiting.

Once Moses came. He arrived secretly, accompanied by only one man, who kept his silence. A boy waited atop a small dune for them to appear and led them wordlessly to the camp.

They were more surprised than impressed by Moses' appearance. It was said that he had killed an Egyptian; that he had fled for his life far across the desert, all the way to the distant Ancestral Land; and that, unapprehended, he had returned from there. Some said that he had two hearts in his breast, one Hebrew and one Egyptian, and that he had murdered the Egyptian one so as to leave no trace of it. Some even swore that they had seen the scar on his chest. Yet although he did not quite seem a Hebrew like the rest of them, there was nothing obviously Egyptian about him either. Egypt was all eloquence and ceremony, whereas he had trouble talking and spoke the Hebrew language quite clumsily. The more slowly he talked, though, the more quickly he paced back and forth while gesturing with his hands, his prognathous beard pointing forward as though he knew his exact destination. He was tall and broad-shouldered, yet seemed ashamed of it, as if he did not want to be a cut above anyone, so that he hunched himself down with a winning, likable modesty. Sometimes an Egyptian word slipped into his speech, causing him to blush all over. He told them that it was time to go.

There were among them, they said to him, some who talked a great deal about returning to the Ancestral Land. Yes, yes, he answered distractedly, as if the point lay elsewhere. The point was to go. All of them. Even those who were still in Egypt. To become one clan, together. Together. He joined his two large hands, as if to show them how closely, how inextricably together he meant.

His Egyptian childhood oppressed him; he was unable to free himself of it. He talked to them about eternity, that of life and that of death, and was forced to resort to Egyptian. He spoke of the mummies by which the Egyptians made death last forever, and of a burning red berry bush in the desert that was deathless life. Although they did not understand him, they nodded politely, without arguing. If the man wanted to talk about burning bushes, let it be burning bushes. Then he asked how many of them could live as shepherds. This was an easier question, one they could readily answer: most of them, they told him, in fact nearly all of them, even those who more recently had worked as builders, or as farmhands, or in the waterworks. The Hebrews are a people of shepherds, they said. They eat the sheep, and wear the sheep, and sleep with the sheep to keep warm. At that his face lit up, as if a more pleasurable reply could not have been imagined; he clapped hand against hand, shining all over, until they were amazed.

After this he took his leave of them and returned with his escort, who still had not spoken a word. The same boy who had brought them led them back to where they could see the long green line that was Egypt. There he halted, spat, and retraced his steps again.

They kept on leaving, and those who had left now formed a large camp. Not all of them lived together. The desert was huge, though scattered about in it were lonely Egyptian farms with cattle pens hedged in by low brick walls and little fields of beans and clover—more gardens really than fields—whose green was flecked with white egrets. The Hebrews kept away from these farms. Here and there half-savage armed guards watched them as they passed, matching stare for stare until they were gone.

One could no longer easily say how many of them there were. The camp swelled with each passing month and year, and a day's walk in any direction brought one to more camps. By day and by night wondrous stories made the rounds. It was said that Moses had had a great fight with Pharaoh himself. That he had vanquished all the sorcerers of Egypt. That his staff had turned into a leopard, a lion, a deer. That he had brought death upon all the firstborn of Egypt. That he had brought plague and pestilence. They themselves were not sure if they believed these stories or not. They told them hesitantly, with a slightly vacant expression that was followed by a short, nervous laugh. They waited. By now there was no returning to the heart of Egypt, yet they knew that they could not long remain where they were. Meanwhile the strange stories filled their days. Baita too, who sat in a corner with Eshkhar in her lap, listened to them avidly. It was rather odd for some of them to hear such tales about Moses, whose mother Yokheved, a woman gone dotty with age, they knew well. Still, no one denied them.

And then they were told that they were setting out.

The grace-light of a broad sunset flooded the land. Flocks of egrets wheeled overhead as if searching for the light's end. Nimbly in the camp below the boys seized the bleating sheep. From out of the houses came voices, bellows, shouts, and croaks. Straw baskets and panniers stood outside, packed and tied with hemp that had run out, so that, by each doorway, people crouched by twos and threes weaving more as quickly as they could. Bundle was piled upon bundle. Women wrapped fruit in broad leaves and tied clusters of dates to long poles. Here and there things were broken in the rush. A smell of roast meat, of blood, of spilled beverage, and of date honey hung in the swiftly darkening air. The trampled, muddy clay paths of the camp glittered in the sunset, and later in the flickering light of the torches, with a gross, dark, bloody sheen. It was almost as if the quick of life itself, now shamelessly exposed for all to see, were being readied for transfer to some other place: the utensils of women thrown about out-of-doors, the now useless guts of sheep, the chamber pots and slop bowls, broken shards, the bare frame of a spinning wheel that never would spin again.

With the first stars the bonfires leaped higher. The time for the paschal sacrifice had come. Hurry, urged the elders, hurry. Swiftly, with light strokes, the knife was wielded and cuts of meat were thrown into the flames by the boys. They ate in haste, standing in front of their houses or at the ends of the muggy lanes, ripping the meat apart with their fingers, which dripped half-raw fat, and smearing it on the walls and the doorposts. Some of the women served large leaves of lettuce and celery to wipe up with. Hurry, urged the elders, hurry. The boys leaped forward to stamp out the fires and scatter the coals. Some made water on the embers. More torches were lit and the camp seethed.

They shouldered their possessions and set out, suddenly

silent, strung out in a long line, the children clinging to the edges of their parents' robes. The lady Ashlil, who had arrived in camp unbeknownst to them, walked erect among them, her large bundles borne by her manservants. The house of Yitzhar shuffled along in its usual disarray, as if it had forgotten or left something behind. Baita walked in its midst, her hand held by Eshkhar, who, barefoot, looked curiously about him, sucking a sugarcane. In the unsteady light the herds and flocks separated each group and household from the others. There were not many torches. A great blackness loomed before and behind them.

The throng kept swelling. Everywhere more people fell in line. Near one of the camps the column was joined by the house of Tsuri, bearing their musical instruments, though they marched now in silence without playing. In bare feet, in sandaled feet, they walked on, over low hummocks and hillocks and dunes, to the clink of their earthenware vessels and the snorts and grunts of their animals. On and on. In the gateways of the scattered farms along the way stood an occasional Egyptian who watched the nocturnal procession go by in astonishment, as silent as the marchers.

By the time dawn broke on the abandoned Hebrew camp thousands of people had passed into the sands and vanished there. A breeze rippled through the thatch of the deserted huts. Here and there along the road leading to the great desert lay bits of broken pottery, strewn fascicles of beans, the sole of a disintegrated shoe.

Clouds of birds and flies swarmed down on the empty camp.

An immense freedom, vast beyond human measure, hung over everything. The days had no rules and the laws of nature themselves seemed suspended. There was no longer any need to rise for work in the morning. There were no masters and no slaves. There was only the desert, which held no threat, and the gullies among the rocks. And the fresh, boundless mornings with the thinnest of mists rising from the thorn trees and from the flowering star thistles in the plain. The silence was palpable. There was no end of sky.

People had lived before them in the plain. Skulls and parts of skeletons, not all of them human, were found in the gullies. Eshkhar hated and feared these bones. Those are day-yed Egyptians, he would say, clinging to Baita, always giving the word two syllables. Baita told him that a dead Egyptian turned into a crocodile or a jackal. His ba and ka came to take his soul and put it in another creature. But a Hebrew didn't turn into anything. He was just buried. In the end some boys took a few sacks, collected these relics, and dumped them far away. One of the younger boys kept a giant jawbone, bigger than any ever seen.

Sometimes, before the break of dawn, someone would awake in a fit of wild joy and roust out all his neighbors. Then the sun would come up on an unwashed, unruly, shimmying camp dancing in great festive circles. They called these days holy days. But they had no need for words. Occasionally, in the middle of the night, as though in a drunken stupor, men would barge into Moses' tent and wake him from his sleep. He should not put on airs. He should not think that this was Egypt. He should not think that he was pharaoh. Sometimes, when he passed through the camp, he was accosted and slapped good-naturedly on the back until his bones nearly broke: we're proud of you, son of Amram, we just want you to know, you may be a stammerer, they may have fished you from the Nile, but we're proud of you all the same, even if we know all about your mother Yokheved and those heathenish teraphim she sits on in her tent like a mother hen on its eggs, you're our boy and we love you, you thicktongue. And Moses, who could not stand being touched, would control himself with a precarious smile, his stammer getting worse, and make his way through the good-humored stench. In those days he considered it important to be seen by everyone. Yet he seldom got as far as the tent of Yitzhar at the hindmost end of the camp. Its dwellers were by no means the most distinguished of the families of Israel.

One day Nun came to Moses. He spoke Egyptian and importuned him greatly, thrusting an obsequious hand into his belt to make him yield. He had brought his son Joshua with him; let Moses take him as his aide and bodyguard to protect him from the crowds that were so lovingly, glad-handedly free with him that soon they would kill him with affection. Moses would rather have declined, but ended up by agreeing. From then on anyone wishing to see him had first to get past Joshua, who sat by the flap of his tent. There was some grumbling, but he was no longer harassed as before.

There were no sounds. A few bleats or whinnies from the

flocks, a few human voices from the gully or the spring, now and then the sharp screech of some bird. All the sounds of settled land had been washed from their ears. The shouts of their taskmasters too.

Baita, make a sound like a water buffalo, Eshkhar would plead. Make a sound like a turtledove. Make sounds like Egypt.

And she would make all those sounds to keep him from forgetting, perhaps to keep herself from forgetting too. They would suddenly come to her, such as a certain stridulation of noontime which, when heard from afar, could be either a roosting rock pigeon, a chirping cricket, or the waterwheel creaking slowly around. A sound of the fields. In low tones she clucked it to him, enchanting both him and herself, her eyes shut as if actually seeing before her the broad green fields of clover and beans that stretched to the far horizon of Egypt.

Every night some fled the camp. They hungered for the greens and the fish, for the mighty murmur of living water flowing serenely down the Nile, perhaps too for the sight of a thin, high-sparred boat skimming soundlessly across a low moon. Without a word they stole back to Egypt. Once a party of five men was sent to the sea for salt. None of them reached it. They returned to Egypt instead, where they assaulted some fishermen and ate the whole catch that was lying in their holds. They wolfed it down raw, bones, guts, and all, fish, mussels, and clams. Afterwards they grew bold and took to thieving in the nearby towns. Within days they quarreled over the gold, and in the end only one of them came back, bringing no salt. It did him no good to protest his innocence. One of the elders raised an angry hand at him and killed him. No more salt parties were sent out.

At night there was fear. No one talked about it. The immense emptiness drove them close to each other, where they lay huddled under a weave of palm shoots. At times they still dreamed that Pharaoh's army had come to look for them in the desert; at times of the green banks and the mud of the Nile, or of Egypt's huge ashlars and statues. Fear alone kept even more of them from returning. In their sleep the entire desert rose to crush them with the most dismal of possible deaths. They trembled with terror and with cold. Each morning the sun was a miracle of redemption. Somehow they never quite believed that it would come again to rescue them from the night.

Baita would tell Eshkhar stories to keep him from running away or from going off to play with the older boys. Yet he could not be tethered anymore. He disappeared for whole days at a time, with Aviel, with Zemer, with Joshua's brother Yakhin, to appear again in the evening like a penitent little animal and lay his head in her lap. Then, as if their bodies were wiser than they and wiser than all words and deeds, their lost peace returned. Once he told her that he no longer believed that there was such a place as Egypt. There was no Ancestral Land either. It was all fairy tales.

Year by year they grew poorer. The clothing taken with them from Egypt was wearing out. They moved from place to place in the desert, hopping back and forth among its few springs, from tamarisk to zyzyph tree, their comings and goings pointless apart from the needs of their flocks. The terrain was rather hilly and very dry, yet they grew used to it. They teamed to find and gather the juniper manna and to keep themselves and their animals away from the poisonously narcotic henbane. The pits from their dates and the dried dung from their flocks were saved to be added to the fires. Here and there they managed to sow, reap, and grind a bit of grain, enough for a bushel or two. Far ahead of them, in front of the camp, a huge bonfire, whose pillars of smoke and of fire were seen clearly by day and by night, was kept burning. No one strayed very far; if one of the shepherds wandered off until the low hills hid the fire from sight, he quickly headed back in a panic as if he had stumbled on some godless place and were now seeking absolution. There was no purpose to their lives. It simply was not Egypt. They had exchanged hard labor for freedom. Slavery was over but nothing else had taken its place. Old folk died and children grew up.

A time came when Yitzhar was seen thinking hard. Then he went to the Ephraimite tents and brought back an Ephraimite with him. They made a few calculations and, in the end, announced to the women that the maiden Baita would be given in marriage to a young Ephraimite named Zavdi, and that the bride price was good.

Eshkhar stood by the entrance to the elders' tent. He was a skinny and not very tall boy about twelve years old. For a long while he waited restlessly, not daring to enter, until someone noticed him and motioned him inside.

He was unprepared for the darkness that reigned there. It was foreign and constricting, a far cry from the vast stretches of sand, the slanting light, and the low thickets of thorn trees; for whereas the household tents were always kept open, this one was shut and turned inward on itself. Tattered rugs covered the ground. Motes of dust swirled in the sunbeams that, like combs of light, fanned stripe by stripe through the joins of the tent cloths. Through the play of dust Eshkhar dimly discerned the faces of several of the elders. Yet they did not look the same as they did out-of-doors, so that he felt as if he did not know them. Standing with his back to him in a corner, pouring buttermilk into bowls, was the man who had signaled him to enter.

Someone asked him for his name and he answered, though so invisible was his questioner that he might as well have been talking to a shade. The man with the refreshment passed through the comb of light, glowing striped for a moment before fading out again, and served the bowls to the elders sitting opposite. Then there was silence once more, followed by a sound of slurping and whispers that Eshkhar could not make out. He stood waiting patiently. The dust danced before his eyes.

Finally he was asked what he wanted.

Something was puzzling him, he replied, something he did not understand. He knew, of course, that there was nothing to the beliefs of the Egyptians, and that the Hebrews did not think that there were any bas or kas who came to take your soul when you died. Yet the question bothered him whether or not one was born again after death, and if so, whether one's next life would be different from this one, or the same.

They were taken aback. Even in the dark he could sense their surprise. Suddenly he felt uncomfortable. He had thought that, being wise men and used to such questions, they must answer them all the time. Now he saw that he was wrong.

Wonderingly they asked him if he had not come to them for judgment: had someone robbed him of a lamb, or had some bread or garment been taken from his tent, or had the man whose flocks he tended done him wrong? Embarrassedly he answered no. Uneasy whispers were exchanged and a new voice inquired why he was asking such a thing. Was it just some riddle he had thought up? No, he said, no; it was more than that. See, his girl, Baita, the daughter of Yitzhar, had been betrothed to another man, and he wanted to know if this life was the only one they would have or if he could look forward to another in which amends would be made and he, Eshkhar, could take her, Baita, for his wife.

He was unprepared for the great peal of laughter that erupted. It started with one of them and spread to the others. Gasping until they were hoarse they bawled into their buttermilk, their beards wagging, the tears streaming from their tired eyes. A lot they had seen and heard in this tent, but never the likes of this. And from whom? Why, from a young pup whose maleness was not yet even half-cocked. Someone has taken his pussy away and he wants to summon God to justice.

Eshkhar spun around and darted from the tent. Crying with anger and humiliation he bounded through the camp, running on and on until he came to where Moses dwelt. He would see Moses. He would tell him about the evil elders. Moses would judge him himself.

Joshua was sitting by the flap of the big tent, his curled side-whiskers gracing his broad moonface like two sentries standing guard. Spotlessly groomed, dressed all in white, he looked with disdain at the thin, grimy boy whose face was smeared with dirt and tears. What brings you to us, he asked with a barely perceptible stress on the last word. Eshkhar replied that he wished to see Moses. Joshua regarded him with a show of patience that was in fact anything but. We are resting now, he said. When we rest there is positively no entry. And after that we have business. Perhaps tomorrow. Perhaps the day after. If the boy would care to tell Joshua his problem, he, Joshua, of little account though he was, might be able to help.

Eshkhar let loose a tirade of words. They poured forth from him in an inarticulate babble, of which all Joshua heard was Yitzhar, Baita, elders, Yitzhar, bride-price, justice, justice, justice. The thinnest of smiles flitted over Joshua's chill lips without passing from them to the eyes, and he said:

—We work miracles. Justice is not our concern.

Whereupon he rose to his feet, his large white moonface filling the boy's field of vision. For an instant Eshkhar longed to poke his fist into its insolence and did not dare; yet Joshua, it seemed, read his thoughts well. Puffing his lips in triumph, he said:

—Go see the elders, boy, they'll justice-justice you all day long. Why, they pull each other's beards out, looking for justice there too. They make you come and go a hundredfold and still they don't find it for you. If the boy knew what was good for him he would take himself elsewhere, because already a gang of loiterers, damn them, was gathering by the tent. Clear out of here right now or we'll be woken from our sleep. Get along with you now, scat!

At the entrance to Yitzhar's tent Eshkhar paused by the hanging gourd to wash his face and gulp great draughts of water. There was no one to help him but himself. And he would have to take Baita by himself, as a man took a woman; then she would be his and could never marry Zavdi anymore.

She was sitting in the tent, languidly waiting for the women to come and prepare her for the wedding ceremony. Anointed from head to toe with an unguinous, aromatic oil, her pomaded hair suffused with a sharp scent, she sat vacantly on a pile of sacks, her embroidered gown and jewelry in a corner, chafing her oiled arms as if to dry them; hearing Eshkhar's steps outside, however, she rose at once. What is it, her frightened eyes asked. But he did not answer. He fell upon her with all his might, embracing her, forcing her to the floor, striving to intertwine their legs; while she, stirred, let herself imagine for a moment that it was all a mistake, that rather than be brought to the house of Zavdi she was about to belong to her Eshkhar, who had grown overnight, as she was always meant to be; even now she was yielding to him with a dreadful sweetness, even now her scented arms were around him and her mouth was open beneath his, clenched and unripe though it was.

But Eshkhar was still a boy. A moment later he pushed her away with a whimper and ran from the tent, ran far beyond the limits of the camp, where he threw himself down in the sand and sobbed as he rolled in it, rubbing against it as hard as he could to expunge what was left of the alien scent, of the last traces of his defeat.

He fled so far that he did not see Baita being brought to Zavdi's tent while the women sang and drummed all around her. Her eyes dilated, slightly drugged by all her unguents, she walked in their midst, hungry from fasting all day and embarrassed by all the commotion. Zavdi was a young man of almost eighteen with a still-unformed face, yet his hands were large and wise. All night long he gathered her to the piping of the flutes outside, the flutes of the house of Tsuri, and to the drumming of the women. Between one song and the next Baita's mother and aunts burst into the tent to seize the embroidered cloth and display her virginity to the guests. Then the merriment waxed even greater and the young men shouted cries of encouragement to Zavdi inside the tent: keep it up, Zavdi, they called, keep it up, you have the whole desert to water, or shall we come in there to help you? while Zavdi laughed heartily in the darkness: perdition take them, from highland to bushy lowland, he would water by himself.

Perfumed, ornamented, aroused, her hungry young body aching, Baita accepted him without question. Somehow it seemed to her that all the celebrating was just for a day or two, after which everything would be the same as before. In the morning, she thought, she would go see what had happened to Eshkhar. But morning found her weary of limb, her hair disheveled like a garden after a storm, with Zavdi deep in satisfied sleep by her side. She played with the scent locket around her neck and went nowhere.

Eshkhar fled to the remotest flocks, grinding his hatred between his teeth. His face was ashen and his movements slow and dreamlike, like a man under water. One day he returned to Yitzhar's tent. He did not so much as glance at the Ephraimite encampment, as if the very direction it lay in had ceased to exist. He wished, he said to Yitzhar, to start his own flock. Yitzhar hemmed and hawed a bit, but he knew the boy was right. Some day he would have to wive, beget, and set up house for himself, without a legal inheritance. Though he strove to drive a hard bargain, so did Eshkhar. He knew now that justice was on the side of the strong. Slowly he built up a flock. Quickly he learned to defend it. Once or twice a ewe with young was taken from him by force. He received blows and returned them. He made himself a big club and pastured far away. And when his friend Aviel came looking for him in the hills, he hid and did not show his face.

T hen came the incident of the Dedanites.

Ever, ever so slowly, so slowly, in the saddles of their gigantic camels, in high, vertical waves, ballooning with each step to the chime of the coins and the tinsel that bordered their harnesses, the Dedanites came riding into the rear of the camp. Even their camels exuded arrogance. The Hebrews stood looking at them from the openings of their meager, scattered tents. They had many saddlebags.

The Dedanites wore flimsy hats with long neckcloths to protect them from the sun. Their beards were rather sparse.

They were heavily armed. The slaves who had followed them on foot leaped quickly forward to seize the bridles and bring the camels to their knees. Cumbersomely the Dedanites slipped to the ground, where they stood amid the loud grunts and belches of their mounts, some ten of them in all, surveying the crowd that had formed in the dismal camp. One of them said something in Canaanite that was not understood. Several of the Hebrews approached. The spokesman waited a moment, then switched to Egyptian. Seasoned travelers that they were, the Dedanites' first request was to be allowed to pay homage to their distinguished hosts' god, if only they might be shown his sanctuary.

The Hebrews had never been so dumbfounded in their lives.

So complete was their bewilderment that they simply reddened and said nothing. The Dedanites waited politely. When no answer was forthcoming they reiterated their great desire to honor the god of their hosts, of whose great powers they had heard in the lands where they traded. Should it be his gracious pleasure they might perhaps sacrifice a slave or two to him, or else make him some other gift, all according to their hosts' custom. At last one of the elders morosely informed them that the god of his tribe was secret and did not show himself. The Dedanites barely managed to conceal their derisive smiles beneath their mustaches. A strange god indeed these people must have, said their faces. Perhaps he had gone to answer nature's call. Perhaps the god of the Hebrews was little and, when sought out, scuffled off to hide in the rocks like the coneys of the desert. But they proceeded with their business.

Verily they had heard that their hosts, the children of Israel, freemen and freemen's sons, had with them the riches of the land of Egypt, which their great and world-renowned god had graciously bestowed on them. If they would be good enough to grant a few days' hospitality, they, the Dedanites, would open all their saddlebags before them, every last one of them. Heaven forbid that they should hold back a thing, no, no, no, they had with them fine weaves, and embroidery, and the fruit of the almond tree, and handsome cookware, and gleaming flint vessels. Perhaps some of these worthless objects might find favor in their hosts' eyes. They would open everything, without exception; for they knew that the children of Israel were not desert brigands, perish the thought, and that not one thread of what they had brought to this distinguished place would be unaccounted for. Indeed, as for brigands, they had already dispatched fierce and powerful ones, whose bones now lay bleaching in the sands. Casually they touched the handles of their daggers as they spoke, an icy glitter in their eyes.

Someone signaled assent. In a trice the camp was trans-
formed. The Dedanites' servants knelt and unpacked large, comfortable tents whose flaps were left opened wide. More and more
onlookers arrived, forming a tight ring around them, curious to
see how they sat and how they ate. The Dedanites, however,
took their time. Only toward evening did one of them clap his
hands, causing the saddlebags to be opened and their wares to
be spread out upon rugs. The Hebrews stared in fascination all
evening without buying a thing. Not until the next morning did
one or two women shamefacedly step forward and emerge from
a tent with a small vial of antimony. The human ring remained
nearly intact.

For four whole days the Dedanites engaged in the minutest
barter, a yard of cloth for some quail eggs dried in sand, a vial
of balsam of hyssop for some date honey, cheaper than any that
could be bought in Egypt. The trade they had come for, though,
failed to materialize. They were certain that the treasures of
Egypt were well hidden in the tents of these Hebrews. They refused to disbelieve in them. If the Hebrews had not plundered
the wealth of the land of Egypt, they insisted in language that
grew less and less ornate, why had they fled from there? Or
could it be that the gold of Egypt had a call from nature too and
was hiding in the desert like their little god, whom they clearly
were ashamed of, since they would not show an idol or an image
of him? They had been dealing in women's trifles, grumbled the
Dedanites, in petty haggling that was not at all what they were
here for. Come, come: where were all the brave men? Where
were the true treasures on account of which they had fled Egypt,
notorious bandits that they were, and eluded their pursuers to
this day?

The Hebrews looked abashedly at each other and did not
know what to say. Never before had it struck them how poor
they really were. So poor that even the flies that had followed

them from Egypt and were once always in the corners of the children's and the flock's eyes had disappeared, as though swept by the wind to some other, less paltry place. There was never a bit of refuse in or around their camp. Any site abandoned by them in their wanderings was left as clean as on the day of Creation, there being not the smallest item, no snip of thread or broken shard, that they did not find a use for. Their lives were as lean as their bodies. Nor did it occur to them to send the Dedanites to any of the other camps. They would only find the same desolation there.

The Dedanites sent a slave to spy the Hebrews out. The man, a most ugly-looking fellow with a low brow and a split upper lip, sought out their company at once. Smiling hideously he told them that he himself was of the seed of Abraham, Isaac, and Jacob, a Hebrew whose distant ancestors had not descended to Egypt. They regarded him suspiciously, with revulsion. They could not abide his friendliness or his smiles, which were all moist red gums amid the hairs of his beard. He followed them around like a sedulous fly, picking up crying babies, helping the women to bear loads, lending a hand with the milking, tying bundles of date pomade for the flocks, and—worst of all—speaking in their own language. He showed some of the men that he was circumcised just like them. Proudly he told them how at night, when the other slaves all knelt to pray to their heathenish idols, he alone remained upright, speaking to God. Just like their forefathers beyond the River Jordan. Like Abraham, Isaac, and Jacob.

They did not know what to make of him.

And then one day, when he had stepped outside the camp to evacuate himself, Joshua's brother Yakhin approached him from behind and, as the kneeling slave turned his ugly, smiling, perpetually fawning face, coolly stabbed him once, then again, in the throat with his dagger and departed. Eshkhar witnessed it all from behind a spreading thorn tree. He shivered a bit, as if with fever, but did not give himself away. He never doubted that Yakhin had every right. He just felt a bit disappointed. Could the deed be as easy as that?

When they found their slave's body, the Dedanites raised a great hue and cry. To replace him, the best slave they ever had, they demanded three young boys from the Hebrews. And the latter had better stop pretending that they were freemen and freemen's sons. Why, the whole world knew that they were simply rebel slaves who had run away from their rightful masters in Egypt, the least of all of Pharaoh's bondsmen, a riffraff that did not even have its own god to bow down to: three slaves for the murdered man and not a whit less.

Yet even as they railed and ranted, the Dedanites knew well enough that they would not get so much as a single boy. The men ringing them closely around may have looked sheepish, sullen, and not especially courageous, but their ranks were drawn tight. Soon enough indeed a screaming Dedanite who had been tearing at his beard while rolling on the ground declared that so excellent a slave as his was worth more than a hundredweight of good copper, half-a-hundredweight of gold, and twelve flasks of honey, or at least no less—and everyone sighed with relief.

There was no bargaining. The Dedanites stalked haughtily into some tents and seized what they could, crying murder all the while. With a special glee they fell upon the house of Tsuri's musical instruments, making off with them as though they had chanced on a treasure hoard. Hardly one was left unpillaged. A pallid lassitude, perhaps the inscrutable taste of guilt, hung over the camp. The incident of the Hebrew slave oppressed them all. The lady Ashlil's menservants hurriedly hid all her gold beneath a carpet on which she lay down, but the Dedanites did not enter her tent.

Quickly they gathered the little they had found and mounted their kneeling camels, which sprang at once to their feet with their riders. Leaving the camp as swiftly as they had entered it slowly, they threatened to inform on it to the first Egyptian garrison they met, which, they said, was less than a day's march away.

The fact of the matter was that the Hebrews could have trailed them easily and taken everything back. But they were too low-spirited. A bad taste, a taste of wrongdoing and defeat, was in their mouths. The last echoing shouts died away. They were alone again, strung out in their ragged camp, in the open plain between the tamarisk and the zyzyph tree, as poor as they had been before.

And yet, thought many of the camp dwellers without saying it, and yet we should have had a god to show them. So as not to be shamed.

Following this they hurriedly left the plain and walked for several days to a country of high cliffs. They marched quickly until, one evening, they made camp opposite a large outcrop of rock. They were off the caravan route and no longer needed to fear pursuit by Pharaoh, but they had left the springs behind too and arrived very thirsty. Here and there they found water in a catchment or in a trickle on a rock-face that was here today and gone in tomorrow's sun. They licked the stones, panting like thirsty dogs. They did not pitch their tents that night but slept wherever they collapsed.

In the morning they rose astounded. They had heard of the mountains of the gods, but these mountains were themselves gods, the shapes and massive forms of a world that could not even have been dreamed of in flat Egypt: little wonder that the gods sometimes spoke from them, whether from a lone bramble or from a mountain itself. Forgetting their thirst, they tilted their heads and gazed upward. Some of the mountains seemed to have been created twice-over: once as the usual dirt hills or soft hummocks dotted with desert shrubs, and then, upon these, steep, perpendicular, tremendous reddish-gray walls like the wrinkled parts of a colossal, nonexistent elephant. At times these precipices made one think of a huge, abandoned work-shop whose sculptor had cast down the debris from his work, which crashed down in fractured blocks and heaps of smashed little flints, all piled together in a titanic disorder. The few thorn trees at their foot looked tiny, no bigger than a man's hand. Suddenly there was a great deal of mountain and hardly any sky; yet the sky between cliff and cliff was the bluest ever seen by them, the essence, the quintessence, of sky. The light too was very strong, a clear, rocky, no longer sandy light. They felt sure that the god of these mountains must be asleep for hundreds of years. Sometimes a huge, stony, wrinkled, half-shut eye could be seen in the rockface; sometimes, it was sworn by some, its lid opened to look at those below. Had only they dared, they most certainly would have offered some sacrifice to these god-peaks, some propitiation for having infringed on their domain. But they were afraid. Here and there, in the days that followed, men and women emerging from their tents would first bow quickly, surreptitiously, to the mountain. They knew, of course, that it was not the God of the Hebrews, but who could be sure? Every little rockfall funneling down its slopes was frightening.

But the mountains remained passive. Little by little the wanderers grew accustomed to both their size and their silence. No longer did they think them sleeping gods; more likely they were great dead ones. Perhaps it was the god of their ancestors who had killed them. The black goats climbed the cliffs blithely, sure-footedly, with the children on their heels. Soon their loud shouts echoed from crag to crag.

All these voices and all this life, though, did not penetrate very far up. There were mountains whose summits were impossible to scale, so high that even the largest birds of prey flew beneath and not above them. The Hebrews were certain that up there, in the highest places, still lived gods who could not be reached. There, way, way up, not a shrub or even a lichen could be seen, and the silence was unbroken by a single bird's call. Sometimes a cloud covered the mountaintop; then the valley beneath it was darkened by shadow and its dwellers paused mutely for an instant or two. Throughout their stay in the high mountains they felt like suffered transients, sojourners who did not really belong. The place belonged to no man, it was the demesne of its own strange gods alone. The horizontal face of Egypt, supine in the sun, was very far away.

Though the high mountains trapped a rain cloud now and then, and there were still some sparse traces of old floods in the canyons, the people were thirsty. Light reigned supreme; the heavens were open doors, open windows of it, eclipsing all lines and contours. They no longer seemed to be living in time but in light alone.

Eshkhar camped by a canyon that still had some water in it, though this had grown brackish and was scummed over by a noxious, darkly iridescent slime. Thirst gripped them all. Each coped as best he could. They no longer boiled their food or even tried roasting it, apart from some rare, wispy little fires of twigs or broom roots that smoked discouragingly and came to nothing. Pale infants clung to their mothers' breasts, barely stirring. The flocks stood still, each ewe's head tucked under the next ewe's belly. At night the thirsty people licked dew from the rocks with their animals; by day they sucked on saltwort and its sharp, unfamiliar flavor filled their mouths. Among themselves they grumbled about this strange place, a place fit for gods but not for men. Their eyes had their fill of fine sights, yet their gullets were parched. In the end they would die amid this feral indifference and their bones would pile up in great heaps. Only the birds of prey would remain. They were waiting already. One afternoon a great sun eagle flew over the camp, gliding slowly, and with a sharp cry let fall a dead woman's arm from its beak. They were struck with dread.

The two women approached Eshkhar in his place far from camp. They walked meekly, downtroddenly, and asked with utter abjectness if he knew of any small catchments that might still have some rainwater in them. They knew, they said, that their family, the house of Tsuri, was far from the foremost of Israel's tribes, yet their infants were sick. Here, he could see for himself the children they were carrying; their breasts were dry and there was no water. Eshkhar looked at them as if impaled on a stake. Only now did he see how the desert had ravaged the house of Tsuri, which had languished more and more since the sack of its instruments. The two women looked barely alive. Why had they come to him, he asked. Why had they not gone to Moses? Let him work them a miracle. He, Eshkhar, was not a miracle man. Did they think that he was Moses that they expected him to restore the milk to their dugs? There were, replied the women, more important people than themselves who had business with Moses; great crowds besieged his tent every day, clamoring for water. They regarded him as they spoke with their large, beaten eyes that were sloe-shaped like those of the whole house of Tsuri's. Each of them hesitantly fingered the skirt of her dress, rolling it back and forth with her free hand. They knew that a man could do only so much.

He said that he would try. That he would look. That he could not be sure. He searched for a long while, scaling with difficulty the high, craggy cliffs, following the calls of the birds. Once or twice a clump of greenery misled him. Finally, after much time had elapsed, he found a puddle that still had not dried out completely. Removing his headcloth, he soaked up all its water and ran back down to the women. They were waiting patiently just where he had left them. Not a word seemed to have passed between them in his absence. The arms of their infants, hot and insentient, dangled down. He handed them the sopping cloth, for which they thanked him submissively; then, tearing it carefully in two, they stuck each half in the mouth of a child and headed back to camp.

The next day the people were told that Moses would bring them water.

They stood, as though in a narrow alleyway, in a white, very deep canyon. One could tell by the birds, which flew low between the canyon walls chattering in loud voices, that there once had been water here. The shrubbery too bore witness to an underground source. Now, however, there was nothing, only a very slow trickle from a single crevice, one drop at a time that took forever to gather and swell until, bursting at last, it cast itself off from the whitish rock and plunged downward. Followed, after a long interval, by another. The walls of the canyon were steep and its floor was littered with flattened white rocks like petrified bedding. There was a smell of dry mold in the air. They stood jammed together at the canyon's bottom end, surrounded by echoes, overhung by a great deal of rock.

Eshkhar stood at the canyon's top end, watching detachedly. The crowd of people was very large. Among the flat rocks were still a few puddles of scummy green water in which the great throng sloshed its feet. Some held empty flasks or water jugs. Soon there would be water. Moses had said so.

The two women whose babies were dying of thirst stood off to one side too. Though the rags from Eshkhar's headcloth were still in the infants' mouths, they no longer had the strength to suck. Most likely the cloth was dry anyway. Red-faced and lifeless, a dark slit of eye stewing beneath each heavy lid like black, boiling mud, they let their little arms hang limply. Their hands already looked dead.

And then, all at once, Moses' party arrived walking quickly. The crowd jostled to make way for it, a highly compact group clad conspicuously in white, squeezed almost shoulder to shoulder with Moses in its midst. His tall staff issued above it like the mast of a white boat that cleft a swift course among the throng.

The group reached the front rock and broke ranks, so that

Moses could take his place at its head. It was Eshkhar's one fleeting glimpse of him, a man with probing eyes and a pugnaciously
outthrust beard, yet now grim and remote. He seemed impatient, as if eager to get on unhindered with the job. From the
rear, as though he were their prisoner, his white-clad escort
closed in on him again.

For a moment, like a craftsman gauging his work, he appeared to measure the thickness and height of the rock; then,
without warning, lifting his staff straight in front of him like a
crowbar, he jabbed the bottom of it down on the white slab between his feet; with which, not even waiting to see what would
happen, the white group spun around as one man and started
back. The crowd, however, paid it no attention, for all eyes were
on the chalky rock. There could be no doubt of it: the slow
trickle increased from one moment to the next, the drops at first
growing larger and more frequent, then joining to form a
threadlike jet that turned almost at once into a real spout of
water.

Jubilantly, exultantly, they ran yelling to fill their flasks and
jugs. A frightful brawl broke out by the rock. The canyon was
very narrow, and in the strife, people were crushed against its
walls. Others pushed, shoved, cursed, struck, and stepped on
each other. Unnoticed, two men were trampled to death near the
outflow. Yet the water kept on gushing as though it had never
done anything else.

In all this commotion the two women were unable to reach
it. Duress had overcome them and left them too weak to fight. In
any case, their babies were no longer alive. Moses and his escort passed by without seeing them. Hopelessly, they stood staring at the wall of flowing water and at the hideous, fatal fracas
taking place there. The infants' arms dangled earthward, obviously dead.

That night heavy clouds hid the stars. A cold, very strong

wind began to blow. Toward morning a downpour fell and rifled all the catchments and water holes. The canyon was flooded. The birds returned to it at sunup, chattering loudly in low flight. The sated bushes and maidenhead ferns glistened wetly.

They buried the dead. The two mothers buried their babies too and returned, without a word, to their daily chores. They had nothing more to say, neither to Moses nor to Eshkhar. They avoided him, as thin and bent as before.

A year or two after this Baita went looking for Eshkhar. Her two children had a stomach ailment and she professed to be going to gather caltrop bark for a remedy. In truth, however, she headed for the furthest flocks.

Eshkhar noticed her almost at once. As usual he was pasturing his flock far from camp, and the form of the woman that suddenly entered his vision, looming enormous on a nearby hill, shook him to the quick. Although she saw him too, she gave no sign of it. She stood opposite him for a while, then went on foraging on the hillside. Eshkhar stared hard at her without moving, flooded by wave after wave of savage emotion.

Then Baita descended the hill and his heart stopped its terrible pounding.

The next day, and the day after that, she came back. Each time, enormous, alone in the world, she appeared on the same hillside, foraged for a while, gazed at him, and disappeared. His nights were sleepless. Bundled in the warm breath and warm wool of his bleating flock, he lay wide awake looking up at the sky of big stars.

After that Baita came no more.

And one day he entered camp on the run, his eyes shut like those of a man plunging into deep water. Mingling with the crowd he made his way past the tents, past the camp of Levi, past the camp of Reuben, pressing swiftly ahead to the camp of Ephraim, his heart ready to burst. He was sure that he would find her. His legs carried him by themselves.

Baita was sitting in her tent, nursing her youngest child; yet without heeding its protests she put it down the moment he burst inside. Panting, he stood facing her. She went to the water jug, from whose neck hung a cup, and poured him a drink that he downed in one gulp, without stopping for breath, holding the cup out for more. She refilled it. This time he drank more slowly, watching her over the rim, his grave eyes dark and deep. He seemed to be all eyes; all-seeing; and he held her eyes with his own as though binding them to him. Her eyelids trembled. She wanted to shut them but could not.

She herself blocked the tent opening with fardels of twigs. Whose if not his could she be?

Afterwards she cried from emotion and a bit from fear too. Eshkhar's temples were alabaster white. He pressed her close and wiped away her tears, promising to take her far, far away. She nodded, not knowing whether she was happy or miserable. Things had become too much for her. Yet even as he spoke Eshkhar knew well enough that there was no place for him to take her and no place for them to go. Beyond the pillar of smoke there was nothing.

Baita was afraid. So deathly afraid that she almost panicked. During their infrequent meetings she took to pushing Eshkhar away from her, her hands shaking, her pupils contracted. Her father and mother would kill her. They would publicly stone her. Zavdi would murder the children. He held her palsied body, weeping with fear, in his arms. Once he even struck her. In the end she confessed that she was afraid of Moses, only of him. He had ways of finding out everything in the world, on earth, in heaven, even in the stones. That was what made her limbs shrink. Perhaps she had been ill all along, or perhaps her illness was caused by her fear. She was a strong woman and fought it for as long as she could. Yet eventually she took to her bed, rivulets of sweat pouring off her, her hands clawing the rug, her feet twitching, until, midway through a spasm, she turned as hard as a rock and was at peace. Zavdi, crying hotly and copiously, brought her to her grave.

Eshkhar went back to his mountain.

He did so because he wanted nothing to do with God. Others had their escapes; for him there was none. His stay in the camp had flayed him alive. Each sickness, each misery, every pain was suffered in his own flesh. If a child was beaten, the beating was given to him; if a man cried at night, the tears were his own. He roamed the camp, an echo of everyone's hurt, until he nearly collapsed. The agony of Baita had become for him the agony of the whole world, and he had no protection against it. He felt that he was going mad in this place. From afar there would be no need to see them all, to think of them all, of every diseased, or blinded, or dying man, of everyone who was oppressed. The fate of Baita and the fate of his mother, Milka, merged for him into one indistinguishable whole. His life in camp had become a horror. Among its dwellers he was vulnerable and exposed, incapable of forgetting, powerless to heal.

At heart he knew that he could not wander far beyond the pillars of smoke and fire, but still he tried. He began to explore the desert a day or two's walk at a time. He found valleys paved with huge slabs of stone like highways; he found canyons in which grew hawthorn and quince trees; he found graves, and temples, and queer manmade structures, and bones. During one of these excursions to nowhere he fell and broke his ankle. Somehow he hobbled back, but the bone knitted badly and left him with a limp. He grew used to knotting a thick rope around it and walking with the aid of it.

Having no friends, he had habits. Every day had its set routine. He no longer desired visitors, who would only get in the way. He stayed or went exploring as he pleased. He found no other gods in the desert. But he did find other destinies.

Once, having climbed to the top of a mountain, he was made to gasp for breath: across the valley beneath him, clearly belonging to someone, set amid a covey of fruiting trees that grew closely around it, stood a house. He waited for darkness to come, then slipped quietly down to it and pressed himself against a crack in a wall. In the large room sat a couple, a man and a woman, their disproportionately short legs folded under them, their rigid faces staring straight ahead. Their chairs were made of a rich, dark wood covered with strange drawings and engravings. In the woman's lap, its eyes shut, lay a cat.

Eshkhar was appalled beyond words. Why then, he thought dimly, all their wandering in the desert, all their misery, all the death from thirst and disease? Hobbling on his bad foot he fled for dear life, running night and day until he rejoined his flock, his ears ringing from the pace and from the insoluble riddle that left him utterly blank. In the end he realized that he would never solve it. He was no longer even sure that he had seen what he thought he had, or that, should he ever go back, he would see it again. The wild notion that things might be otherwise faded and died away. Once more the desert closed in on him. He grew deeper into himself.

Not once did he dream of Baita. It was as if she had journeyed far away from him, so far that there was no telling where.

So that, returning one day with some newborn kids in his arms, he was startled to find, their hair grown wild, Aviel, Yakhin, and Zemer sitting and waiting awkwardly for him outside his tent. They embraced, then jostled each other a bit as they had done when they were children, until each came to rest on one foot, from which they vehemently continued their bumping, hopping about like chickens and laughing helplessly.

Aviel was the first to collapse on the ground, followed by Zemer; soon after which all four of them lay in one heap, wiping their eyes. Then they rose and trooped into the small tent. Eshkhar was embarrassed to have nothing to serve them. If only they would wait a bit, he would go fetch a kid, milk a goat. But they had not come for that, they said; they had come for a word with him. In the tattered tent with its habitual reek of dried-dung fuel, goat hair, and broken wind they told him that he was smarter than any of them, that he had known, cunning rogue that he was, just when to leave the camp. Now every man jack of them was set to leave too. Moses had gone off somewhere, no one knew for how long, while Joshua sat at the entrance to his tent lording it over them all. For some time the people had been saying that they had had enough of wandering about the desert at Moses' beck and call, one day to the lowlands and the next to the highlands, now to die of illness and now of thirst, never knowing the where or the why of it. They were turning into a shameless mob, like the first castaways who had left Egypt long before them. They were all castaways now.

—We came forth from Egypt, said Aviel in his soft voice, we came forth from Egypt, Eshkhar, we left the house of bondage, and now we are pining away in this desert and are going to die in it. Why, even if Moses wanted the whole generation that left Egypt to be killed off here, it's the children who are dying in our arms, not the old men. We've dug more graves than we can count, and there's still no end in sight.

And Zemer added:

—We must honor our children that their days be long upon this earth. The people are stealing from each other's tents, Eshkhar, it's like a plague of locusts in the camp. Men have even been murdered because of it. But we shall not steal nor murder. And none of us shall rule another or tell him when to work and when to rest. Because that's why we left the house of bondage, so as not to be slaves anymore. And there shall be no lies among us. Only if each man loves his neighbor will there be peace in our camp.

Eshkhar asked what they would do if the people did not let them go. We shall have to wait and see what we do then, said Aviel uncertainly. Though Yakhin says that we will smite them.

Eshkhar glanced at Yakhin. He sat muscular and taciturn, playing with his short dagger and gazing tranquilly back as if to confirm the execution of the harelipped Dedanite slave. If the people do not let us go, said his perfectly still eyes to Eshkhar, then they are a people of slaves and will be cut down just as he was. Did you not see for yourself how easy it was to kill?

Aviel, though, sought to temper things, to be vague, to say nothing so outright that it left no room for retreat. There were so few of them, he said. Most of the people were so much grass to be trampled on. They rose like dumb animals, and went to bed like dumb animals, and were led about from mountain to mountain like dumb animals by Moses, on and on and on. That was why the three of them had come to Eshkhar. They wanted to ask him to come down to the camp with them at once, before Moses returned, since as soon as he did the people would follow him again like mooncalves, even right into their graves. Now is the time, they said. And headed back.

Warily, cautiously, gradually, Eshkhar moved his flock back toward the camp, advancing a little each day. Already he could clearly see and hear the hubbub of life at the foot of the high mountain. The winter was over. The canyons were full of water and the valley had sprouted everywhere with patches of green. Countless flowers covered the hillsides: bean caper, and stinkweed, and yellow primroses, and the fierce purple of the henbane. The people had risen from their former dejection; the curtain of despondency that had accompanied them from Egypt seemed to have lifted. The valley hummed as if each pair of hands was busy looking for something to do, as if many thoughts, songs, wooings were circulating through it. That winter, for the first time in their lives, they had seen and been terrified by the snow in the high mountains. Most of the graves on the bottom slopes were of children and infants who had died from the cold. The night frosts had gnawed at them mercilessly. Now the sun warmed their bones and straightened their spines, and with it came a surge of new strength.

Eshkhar felt restored too. The people he met when he finally came into camp were happy to see him, as he was to see them. He ate real, honestly ground and baked bread. Disheveled, chastened, he sat with his friends thinking what a fine fool he had been. Why, he was flesh of their flesh.

They were not alone in their discontent. Elsewhere, in other tents, groups of men had formed too, some of whom were even thinking of breaking away and returning to Egypt. Of kneeling before Pharaoh and begging forgiveness. Anything was better than this pointless wandering. The camp was full of rebellion. Only the castaways, as usual, laughed unbelievingly. It won't get you anywhere, they said. You had better get used to it right now. Moses will cook you all for breakfast when he gets back and still have room left for dessert. When asked with whom they would go should one of the tribes head off on its own, they replied: with Moses and the Levites, of course, they have the sharpest knives. They laughed and laughed. Their laughter grew to be unbearable.

Now Yonat, sister of Aviel, a twitch-faced woman, squatted with them also by the entrance to Aviel's tent. Sometimes she puckered her brow, giving her a sourish look; other times she opened her mouth wide or tilted her head to one side while nodding up and down as though chewing; always, though, her eyes were big, and worlds came and went in them as she listened to the men talk. She herself, born mute, had never been heard to utter a word; yet they always knew what she felt, for her emotions seemed to emanate through her black dress with a fiercely domineering smell. She had in her the power of all pent-up things. Though they ignored her presence, they were strongly aware of it. She always sat on the ground by the tent flap, very quiet and intense.

All at once Yonat leaped from her squat and tore the earrings from her ears, the right lobe's with her right hand and the left lobe's with her left, both in a single motion. Very quickly now, her ears bleeding, she ran from man to man, from woman to woman, her feet skimming into tents and down paths, her gory earrings held out in one hand, mutely demanding, mutely seizing their gold, hurdling tent pegs and tent stays, impatient of ties and clasps, into tents, down paths, her hand extended, making dark sounds in her throat. As a man running with a lit torch sets all around him on fire, so did Aviel's twitch-faced sister Yonat run quickly, setting the camp on fire with a dark, unholy flame. No one dared resist her. No one had the strength to match hers. Perhaps the spirit of the god of the mountains had entered into her. A few women ran to hide from her; yet by now she was trailed by a retinue of men who themselves stripped the indignantly screaming holdouts of their adornments. The gold was brought to the center court of the tribe, where, like some precious scrap metal, it lay on a sheepskin in a jagged, angular pile, gleaming with its own amassed insolence.

They gathered round the sheepskin. The pile was small, barely a few fistfuls of gold. They stood staring at it, as if forced to realize just how paltry their wealth was, just how puny their strength, when the lady Ashlil, her face old and naked without its jewelry, suddenly appeared with a large straw basket and emptied it over the pile. They were overjoyed to see that her gold covered all of theirs.

Stark against the rocks in her black dress, her gory ears a red trickle, Yonat ran quickly through the valley to the tents of the neighboring tribes. There too a great uproar broke out. The day was still young and the sun still high overhead when several men flushed with excitement came to take the gold to the main pile by the great fire at the front end of the camp.

Things had got out of hand. The day's chores forgotten, they stood uncertainly in the openings of their tents listening to the distant stir. Some, making up their minds with a sheepish shrug, slipped off to see for themselves the huge blaze in which the gold was being melted down. A strong smell, a great deal of smoke, and an uneasy sensation, as of some planned festivity gone awry, hung over the camp. Absently the women ran their hands over their legs denuded of anklets and bangles. All of a sudden there was an unaccustomed, a springlike, a disquieting lightness in the air. Without a god, without a leader, they inhaled smoke and waited.

Eshkhar heard the tumult from afar and limped hurriedly into camp on his lame leg, wondering. At the canyon's end he met Aviel, who, flushed and good-humored, hugged him mollifyingly around the shoulders: there's no harm in it, Eshkhar, no harm. Let the people have their day. Tomorrow we shall be the wiser.

The blood rushed to Eshkhar's head. Overflowing with anger he strove to slip free of Aviel's grasp, which only, however, grew stronger: no harm in it, Eshkhar, no harm, a spirit got into Yonat. No one could stop her, she swept everyone with her. And up there, by the column of smoke, there was a miracle, a real miracle, Eshkhar. When all that gold was melted down, it came out looking like an ox. Maybe it's Chemosh. No one touched that gold with his hand, Eshkhar, and still it turned into an ox. It has to be a miracle. You can't fight miracles, Eshkhar!

Panting like two evenly matched wrestlers in the streambed, they stood for a long moment in a frozen embrace, muscles strained, necks crimson, brows bulging, until Eshkhar fought loose of Aviel's stranglehold, threw him violently to the ground, and ran back, containing his limp until he was over the hill. Aviel picked himself up and ran quickly to the fire, where he was swallowed up by the crowd.

Thick smoke and loud cries spread out over the desert, above which wafted a smell of great unease. Eshkhar ran back to his tent and lay down there, burying his sweaty face in his sheepskin. He knew now that his life would be lived out without them, just as theirs would be lived out without him. This was the first and would be the last time that he had betrayed his own solitude. They had sought to seduce him with their freshly baked bread and the treacherous swamp of their friendship, and he had almost let them succeed.

He groaned and gnashed his teeth, squirming where he lay. Back there a few flutes were wailing and men and women, the last survivors of the house of Tsuri, were singing; all evening long, far into the night, sheep were slaughtered to the muffled beat of drums and the billows of reveling smoke. Nowhere in the whole desert was there any escape. A band of raucous youths passed near his tent, howling as they ran. Later a couple that had slipped away from camp came to look for a trysting place and found one not far from him; tormented by their moans and whispers, he could not stop his ears. Tossing on the ground, whimpering to himself like a dog, he lay totally alone in the world.

But there too the revelry turned to groans. The sky had yet to pale when fierce brawls broke out, at the center of which were the bedaggered sons of Levi. Before dawn broke, large groups of unarmed men began fleeing to their tents with cries of horror, leaving hundreds of mutilated bodies behind them. It was later said that Joshua himself ran his brother Yakhin through. A pallid sun rose to shine on the many corpses, on the gnawed cattle bones by the fire, on the overturned pots, and on the wilted flowers drooping from the golden idol that no longer looked like anything at all. It was difficult to fathom how anyone could have thought it an ox or a calf. A cracked silence reigned. Dragging bowed legs, her clothes in tatters, her mouth askew, Yonat was the last to stagger back to the tents at the rear of the camp.

Moses returned to find a gray, extinguished camp that had shut itself up in its tents and did not care to remember what had happened.

They buried their dead and submitted to the Law.

From that day on Moses too seemed a cleft man. At last he told them that they were going to the Ancestral Land. Sadly he spoke to them of blessings, of curses—all, all of which they accepted as though it were their daily bread and they, his day laborers, were hangdoggedly taking it from his hands. They could hardly look each other in the eye. He talked on about olives, about grapes, about pomegranates, about figs, and wearily they answered yes, yes, anything you say, as long as we don't all have to drop dead in this desert, amen. No, they would make no more statues or graven images. Yes, they would not murder. They would not bear false witness. Whatever he told them, amen.

But Eshkhar knew none of all this. He had struck out so far on his own that the pillars of smoke and of fire were no longer in sight, nor did he wish them to be. The camp could go its way and he would go his. He had no notion where it was headed, if it was headed anywhere at all.

For many years, perhaps ten, perhaps more, he wandered by himself in the desert, alone with his flock. If the others crossed it once, he did so dozens of times. And he knew things that they did not: that the desert was inhabited, that it had limits, that it could be crossed from end to end in a matter of weeks. The deception of miracles was keeping them purblind and lost.

Often he took his flock grazing to the north, near the caravan route. Once he saw a party of Dedanites. Though he thought they were the same traders who had plundered them soon after they left Egypt, he could not be sure. There came back to him the memory of the harelipped slave, and with it a heavy, obscure grief. He would have given a great deal to be able to bring that man with his ugly red lip, his fawning smiles, and his dexterous hands back to life. A man should die for his own sins alone, he told himself, knowing that that would never be. Not even with God. It was too easy to kill, to knife, to send disease.

Now and then he saw detachments of Pharaoh's troops clattering loudly toward one of the forts that lined the way. He never hid from them, yet they paid him no heed. Once a caravan passed quickly by bearing the murderer of his mother, the Canaanite overseer, now great and wealthy, who was on his way back to Canaan. But Eshkhar did not know this. He saw only a rich man—some lord, no doubt—with his face concealed from the burning sun, and many slaves. They galloped by, kicking up great clouds of dust. Had they stopped to ask him for water, he would surely have drawn it for them from the well.

From God there came no accounting, neither by day nor by night, when the huge stars hung in their orbits overhead. Sometimes he thought that he was God himself. Once he traveled far to the east and knew without being told that he was in the Ancestral Land. He asked for the name of an oasis and was answered Beersheba, the Well of the Oath. When he went southward from there, descending more and more until he felt sure that he had reached the bottom of the world, he found a slate-colored sea whose odd waters smelled of sulfur. Marveling greatly, he returned. And yet that too was not the world's end.

None of this was known in the camp. They wandered on. No one asked anymore why they lingered so long in the desert.

No one knew why they camped in one place for two weeks and in another for two or five years. If no rains fell, they sowed in dry ground and pounded the meager yield into a coarse flour. It was hard to imagine that there once had been a world apart from this desert, their only home, their only love, their birthplace and burial ground. Most of those who had left Egypt were no longer alive. The others, like doorless and windowless houses, had no other memories. Life in the desert consumed them utterly and left nothing over. Was there really anyplace else? One might see a bronzed youth grab a ewe, grip her tightly by her thin legs, sprawl out with her on his chest, and drink straight from her udder. Who needed a bowl? The women scolded them, but they just laughed and kept on. Theirs was a carefree generation. Instead of memories they had the new law. It never occurred to them to challenge it. If asked, they would have answered: it is a good law.

Once they came to a shore with a very flat sea, and a salt marsh, and open spaces, and feathery rushes, and a beatitude of date palms, and soft, soft surf that spilled onto the sand with warm whispers, a balm for body and soul. In the shallow water stood a jungle of mangrove trees, their roots thick and exposed like the ropes of a fisherman's nets. A kingfisher stood with its head in the water, unafraid. It felt good to be out of the rocky clefts and canyons and to stretch out peacefully with no other sound than the softly sighing surf, or sometimes the splash of a springing fish as it broke water, or the thin, barely audible scrape of the translucent little crabs tracing a line in the foam. The camp eased itself down in great silence, breathing in and out with the breath of the sea, filling its lungs, its whole self with it, letting the blessedness course slowly through it with each hushed pause between wave and wave.

For two or three weeks they immersed themselves in the

murmur of the sea, the soughing of the date palms, and the abundance of fish; then they gathered their possessions and headed back into the maw of the desert. All of them, that is, except for a few remaining families of the castaways, who told Moses that they were staying right here, on this shore. They were not meant, they explained apologetically, for so much governance and laws. His "Thou shalt not steal" was too much for them. They had better stay where they were and not spoil the order of things.

The others pushed on. Long afterwards they remembered that shore with longing, until it too ceased to be a shore in space and became one in time, which they would always seek to return to and would never be able to find. Another year passed and it was no longer even mentioned.

And then one day Eshkhar, slowly climbing a hill, saw the pillar of smoke in front of him.

Gingerly he edged nearer, careful to pitch his tent at a safe distance. He had not seen them for years and could not now prevail upon himself to flee at once. He would, he decided, observe them for a few more days, another week, then move on before he was noticed. Yet more time went by and he remained, standing thoughtfully at the pillar of smoke by day and at the pillar of fire by night, telling himself every day that tomorrow he would be gone. The next day, though, he was still there.

Once, returning to his tent, he noticed a new smell. He looked about and, to his surprise, saw that someone had cleaned his rugs and cooking pots and wet down the floor of the tent. The strange smell gave him no peace.

The same thing happened the next day and the day after that; each day the strange smell of camphor wood clashed with his own stench and the reek of the broom-root coals until the new smell vanquished the old. On the fourth day he spied the woman slipping away from his tent. He overtook her easily and dragged her back with him. She looked at him without fear. As he made her yield he saw that she had six fingers on each hand. She was not a virgin.

She told him that her name was Dina and that, like him, she lived outside the camp and not in her father's tents; indeed, she did not even know who her father was. Slowly, gently, she undid the rough rope that had bound his ankle for years and massaged the bone; then she brought wet leaves and tied them in its place. He himself had made such poultices for his flock and, grumbling a bit, submitted to her fingers. Yet he did not permit her to spend the night in his tent. At sundown she rose without a word and went back to where she had come from.

That night, for the first and last time, he dreamed of Baita. She stood smiling at him as if all were forgiven, as if to let him know that everything was all right. Then, leaning toward him to kiss him farewell with an utter, peaceful finality, she vanished. He woke crying hard.

Dina came back. A few days later she told him in her low voice why she lived outside the camp. She had, she said, conceived out of wedlock and was afraid to go back; if he would testify that she was his wedded wife, she might live; otherwise she was as good as dead already. She spoke perfectly calmly, as calmly as she folded her strange hands that had six fingers on them. When he replied gruffly that she could tell them whatever she wished, she kissed his hands with joy. Sometimes she bent over him and wrapped him in her long hair as though it were a tent.

Once he asked about her fingers. She said she was born that way, to a father whom she did not know, which was why she was considered impure; it was an act of mercy, she had been told, that she was not killed at birth, though she herself sometimes wondered about this; for because of it she had been given to no one in marriage, albeit a certain man from her tribe, a kinsman of hers, or at least so he claimed, had lain with her from time to time until he had got her with child. Observing her, Eshkhar noticed for the first time that her deep-set eyes had the beaten look of the house of Tsuri's eyes in the desert. Perhaps she was all that remained of it. No one had taught her to play music, though. Nor would there have been anything to play it on.

Another time he asked her about his friends Aviel, Yakhin, and Zemer. She told him what she knew: that Zemer was alive and well and the father of many children, and that Aviel had died in battle. He had not even known that there had been a battle, and said nothing for a long while.

When her belly began to swell, she went away. He did not go down into the camp to look for her.

Once more they were on the move. A party of scouts returned with some grape leaves and raisins. They told of huge grapevines that bore wondrous fruit, and of others, fed by a great spring, that scaled high walls. Slowly they began to believe that there was an end to their trek. That the Ancestral Land existed. Once some young men brought back a few olive branches that moved the lady Ashlil to tears. Taking them, she pressed them to her heart. At last, at long last, she said, she had seen the branch of the olive tree; never had she thought that she would live to see the day. All her life she had wanted to see one just once. Jugs of olive oil she had seen, but never a real branch. Now she could die content.

Dina returned with a child in her arms. Watching her sit quietly nursing it, Eshkhar felt a deep peace. He knew that with peace, compassion would come back too, but he no longer had the strength to fight it. One day Dina threw away the rope with which he kept retying his ankle. You don't need it anymore, Eshkhar, she said. He tried taking a step or two and saw that she was right. When winter came with its cold and fierce winds, she took to sleeping in his tent with her son, nor did he turn her out anymore. Once he asked her tauntingly, what about the miracles, were there still many miracles in camp—to which, after mulling it over, she answered that, although she was not sure, it seemed to her that, at least as far as she remembered, the miracles had stopped long ago. They simply had kept plodding on.

Then she conceived Eshkhar's child and, when her time came, went down to the midwives in camp and gave birth to Yotam. And an auspicious birth it was.

Toward the end time itself seemed to go mad and the days and nights chased each other faster and faster. They marched quickly and covered distances greater than any they had covered before. The terrain was rolling now, almost open, and the Land was nearer every day. They no longer had the patience for the routines of desert life, and seldom even pitched their tents when they camped at night. More often they simply curled up in their woolen sheepskins and slept under the sky. The women stopped weaving, the old men gave up making baskets. Their belongings were rarely unpacked. Were it not for the elders, who counted each day and religiously kept track of the holy days, they would have lost all sense of time. In the sky, upon the rocks, in the thickets of thorn trees, they could now make out the birds of a cultivated land.

Gradually, almost imperceptibly, the pillar of flame had been dimming. It burned less brightly and, like a candle in the dawn, had lost its luster. Glancing at its smoldering edges, they felt no grief. They knew that the Land was close by now; those who had pushed ahead of the camp had even glimpsed it beyond a rift-valley whose bottom was too deep to be seen, a long range of mountains that ran the whole length of the horizon, covered by a gray haze. As they approached, the haze turned purplish brown, sometimes almost gold, as though bathed in heavenly grace.

More and more people were pressing ahead to see now, as if they were standing on the deck of a ship nearing land, which loomed larger the closer they came. And yet it was hard to say if they were progressing toward it or if it were coming to meet them, so massive, so majestically colored, though its details were still undivulged.

Not only had the pillar of flame begun to fade. Moses too was no longer the man he once was. His mind was failing. Sometimes, imagining that ba and ka had come to take his soul, he harangued them that he was a Hebrew, not an Egyptian, and that they should go somewhere else. Sometimes he shouted that he must, must enter the land and that no force in heaven or on earth could stand in his way. In his more lucid moments he sought to impose more and more laws on them, a never-ending Torah. Yet even his intimates no longer bothered to write them down. They knew that his hour was nigh; one way or another, everything was already up to Joshua.

Several of the tribes were by now in the Land. No one knew exactly how the order of entry was decided. Those who had entered in the first or second year, it was said, had already fought several wars. The others had to wait.

Eshkhar kept back. The Land stretched out before him along the horizon. He stared at it as if seeking to pierce its misty veil, to make out houses, trees, and wells, but it was too far. He had been standing like that a long time when, as though awakening into a dream, he sensed a strange presence behind him, unfamiliar yet perfectly clear. An indefinable fear kept him from turning around.

Baita? he wondered out loud. But it was not Baita. Something, someone, was calling laughingly to him from the wind, from the mountains, perhaps from the long-remembered years of wandering, someone smiling and forbearing who expected something of him without his knowing what it was. No, it is not the quail, Eshkhar, nor the manna, nor the water from the rock, called the strange presence, which was perhaps only a gentle and belated insight; it's none of these, not even Moses himself; you are close now, Eshkhar, very close; just one more little effort and you will understand.

But he could not understand. He rubbed his eyes, no longer sure that anyone, or anything, had been there. Nor, when he turned around, was there anything except the soft sandstone hills falling away to the desert. He shook his head, as if trying to rid himself of a bothersome thought; then, all at once, like a man who has not done so for years, he began to laugh.

He was heard by Yotam, who had been sent by his mother with a message. Doggedly the boy clambered up the slope, bearing down hard on his bare feet, until his father bent toward him and helped him up the last bit. Dina wanted to tell him that tomorrow the last of the camp was crossing the Jordan. She wished to know if he would come with them. And Eshkhar nodded that he would.

The boy started back down; quickly, though, Eshkhar collected himself and slid after him, taking him by the hand and returning with him to the camp. He stayed with Dina that night. The children pressed their little bodies against him. Dina snored a bit where she lay. Yet all his thoughts, and the many people packing, tying knots, and talking in the moonlight, kept him from shutting his eyes. He had told no one that he had already been in the Ancestral Land.

At last their turn came to enter.

They kept on crossing the river, household after household, family after family, men, women, and many children, those born in the desert and those who had walked all the way from Egypt. They crossed over in good order, helping each other, the good, the bad, the cruel, and the indifferent, the law-makers and the law-abiders. The flocks crossed tied to long poles, bleating with fright. A few lambs that were tied too loosely were swept away by the current. Someone lost a sandal in the river, bent to retrieve it, slipped, fell, and was stepped on by two men bunched close behind him who could not stop in time; at once, however, he was helped back to his feet. The current was strong. Some women lost their bundles, which were carried away downstream, but kept going. The ford was uneven: in places the water was shallow, while in others it rose without warning nearly waist-high. And still they crossed, a living, unswerving river of mankind bisecting the river of water. Aviel's daughter crossed, and the house of Yitzhar, and Zemer with all his large household. Two young men bore the lady Ashlil, sitting up, tightly bound to a litter, cadaverous, bald, her tiny face wrinkled and old. No one knew for sure whether she had died long ago and this was only her corpse, or whether there was still a remnant of life in her.

They kept on crossing. Those in front were already on the opposite bank, the corners of their garments knotted tightly around their waists, their brown legs gleaming with water. Like a flock of long-legged river birds they stamped hard on the sand to shake off the drops, each of them making a small puddle. Then they wrung out their clothes.

And still they kept on. Those who had crossed now stood in a broad, spacious plain whose light was white and expansive. Beyond it rose soft hills that seemed wrapped in a fine, wrinkled silk of a color sometimes white, sometimes eggshell, while set further back were slopes with green growth leading up to a towering wall that they would yet have to climb. They could sense that beyond that high ridge were more mountains, but that it was no more than a short march to the last mountain of all, to the end of all their journeys.

Far to their right stood a city, a place of many date palms splashed with the luxuriant red flowers of a tree they failed to recognize. It was all so new, fresh and sparkling. Their senses swooned before the sudden shock of oleander and flame trees, bees and turtledoves, the strong odors and the barking of the dogs. Some of them looked covetously at the inhabited city. Yet none dared reach out to pluck a single flower or fruit. The black goats alone had already plunged headlong into the bushes, which they started to devour until rounded up. There were butterflies. There were low-flying birds plummeting among the fruit trees. The people looked and looked, dumbstruck, and still they could not look enough.

Afterwards, like beads falling off a string, first two, then three, then five of them broke away from the crowd and nimbly began climbing the mountain. The others followed. The flocks trotted beside them, waves of scent washing over their flared nostrils.

And when the first of them were over the ridge, no one was left in the desert.

PROPHET

The ways of the world began to turn upside down about one hour after sunrise. Herds of livestock that should have jostled through the narrow gate, spilling like a slow sea upon the hills, were seen to stop in their tracks, while distant shepherds turned suddenly, rounding up their flocks, and headed back into the city. Quickly they drove, frantically, with much brandishing of staffs, as if the day had been cut short and evening came abruptly, while the light was still new, and the sun warm in the east.

From the gate rose a din of shouts and shoving. Herds mixed with each other and blocked each other's way, some struggling to get out, others clamoring to get back in, cow haunch pressed against sheep flank, in a great teeming vortex. Thick clouds of dust soared all along the ascent to Gibeon, rising very high, as if the earth had suddenly tilted and the road stood up in the air. Cries of shepherds and lashings of prods cut through the continuous bellows and bleats. Kids and lambs were crushed beneath the baffled hooves of jammed cattle, their loud, desperate calls crying doom.

Here and there, on the fringes of the vortex, a few sheep and calves broke free of the dense cluster, and stampeded up the narrow streets, fleeing the tumult and the shouting shepherds, whose staffs failed to make way among the heaving flesh. The city wall was invisible. Scanty light filtered through the swirling columns of dust, sickly, yellow, and apocalyptic.

Worried Gibeonites looked on from the wall and the rooftops. The city was built on the flat top of a steep hill overlooking a fertile, generously sprawling valley of trellised grapevines and olive, pomegranate, and carob trees, beyond which lay the land of the Jebusite. It was from there, the Gibeonites told themselves mournfully, it was from the east, from the desert, that the evil would come. They were already said to be close, very close. They might even be behind those straggling sheep, picking off the last strays. Was not that the glint of their spears in the distant dust? The shepherds had seen them with their own eyes; ask the shepherds. A people come upon us from the desert. There would be war. There would be a siege.

The voices dropped to anxious whispers. Get everyone inside the gate, they said, get everyone inside and bolt it shut. As if by themselves, their hands described little, worried, enfolding movements.

Children who had awakened and gone outside stood staring openmouthed at the changed world. Everything was diminished, gathered in on itself. The gatekeepers strove in vain to swing the great gate shut and drive home the corner bolt. The square was waist-high in animals. Slavering cows, rancid-fleeced, burr-infested sheep, the whole apprehensively lowing swarm of life, had brought the fields into the fieldless town. The marketplace, with its large, worn paving stones, the edges of the pool by the water tunnel, which should have been crowded at this hour with launderers and water drawers, were now one quivering mass of beast, dense with heat and smells. Swarms of flies accompanied the animals with an unearthly buzzing, whining and taut like many bowstrings endlessly twanged. Barefoot children pressed into the alleyways, caught up in the squirm of herds. The clowns among them hiked up their tunics and danced with the sheep and cows, bare buttocks rubbing against them, hips gyrating obscenely, faces twisted in laughter, wild with wonder and fright.

Finally the gate was shut halfway, and the living sea backed up into streams, each quickly flowing off into another alley. The square emptied out. Only the sound of tremulous bleating still came from everywhere. Several lambs lay crushed upon the ground among fresh droppings, covered by flies as if by a coat of glistening black fur. The dust settled and the sun shone brightly again.

Hivai wiped his face with the back of his broad hand and descended from the wall. Four of the city elders climbed down heavily with him, supporting themselves on a bowed fig tree that grew from where it had sprouted in the stones of the wall. At once a small band of men surrounded them, some talking quickly, close enough to grip the elders' girdles, others squinting off into the sunlight, too abashed to meet the elders' eyes. The city held no pasture. It held no vegetable gardens. It had no garrison. What should a man do that he might live?

It was so. Even the vegetable patch at the foot of the wall had long been neglected and overgrown by thistles. No one had threatened Gibeon for ages. It was a city as large as a royal capital and it had forgotten what fear was like.

The elders listened and kept silent. They seemed to have no words left. Though they said nothing to Hivai, their quick glances at him were sharp as swords. Prophesy, Hivai. Prophesy, man. Isn't that what you were made for? Speak and tell us what a man should do that he might live, so that we can tell all these people.

Hivai stared at the ground. There was no prophecy in him. The elders' unspoken words struck at him like fists in a bitter, discouraging complaint. Why, they knew very well that he could not prophesy to order. He himself never knew whence his prophecy came or whither his prophecy went. It might fail him for years at a time or come to him twice in one day. Expert at such things though he was, he augured neither by the flight of birds nor by the entrails of sacrifices, nor by the bladders of the muscular fish that the Philistine brought on his she-ass in waterskins from the coast. Nor did he tell fortunes with molten wax poured on water; nor with bowls of wheat sprouts, as did the soothsaying women. All these came from the little gods, from the Asheroth perhaps, or from the virgin sycamore on the outskirts of town whose fruit had never been slit. Everyone knew its powers. Enfeebled men seeking succor came to it from all over the mountain land, cheered on by its horde of sanctuary harlots.

But prophecy such as that which had come to him, a man in his middle forties, no more than nine or ten times in his life, was not from these. Perhaps it was from the great gods of the north, the gods of Mount Lebanon; perhaps from gods even greater, the gods of the great rivers, beyond which there was nothing, of that far world-root where dwelt the Fathers of All. Yet this too was far from certain. When it came, it was as if a door opened wide and he could remember the future, could recall it as exactly as if it had happened no more than a moment ago. Once he felt that he was earth, all-earth and all-earth-growth, whereupon he remembered with very great awe that there would be a drought. Another time, with a single sharp pang of his flesh, he knew the pain and sickness that would betide every plague-ridden house in the city—knew it while his chest was filled with a great weeping that would not be wept for many days.

When he knew, he told the elders. When he did not, he said nothing. The elders listened thoughtfully. They knew his prophecies always came true.

He would have withstood torture again, if only it would do some good. Years ago, when he was young and did not know his own strength, he had let himself be brought to the temple and forced to prophesy there. He had been plied with wine, with pestled drugs, with incense, with fasts, with sharp rods that tore at his body. And yet he had hardly felt them. Being in the dark, airless temple, which was like being at the bottom of a pit suffused with the smell of blood and smoke, had paralyzed him with fear. At times, through the clouds of incense, he had made out a small child brought to be sacrificed, crying as it held out its arms to its father. He knew he should know who it was and what it meant, but he never did. Sometimes he thought it a fiction, a figment of his own terror, and sometimes, dredged from deep within him, he thought he could remember a fair five-year-old boy whose name he had forgotten, though once he had played with him in the sunshine before losing him in this darkness. Each time he entered the temple, he was sure it had really been so, and that soon, in the next day or even hour, it would come back to him. Yet each time he stepped back into the street, he was no wiser than before. They saw the bafflement in his face, the torment to know, and persisted. Prophesy, Hivai. Prophesy, man. Their low, muffled voices weighed him down. To remember. To know. To remember. To know.

This time, too, he would have undressed without a murmur, baring the long welts of flesh that were left on his back from those days. He had never protested; he had submitted to the rack as if desiring it, so great was his longing for the moment of prophecy, for that opening forth in which the memory of the future became clear. Apart from these rare times of liberation, his life had the plodding gait of an ox that walks the straight furrow of time from the Was to the Will-be. Even when his torturers despaired of him, he continued sordid self-torments of his own in the hope of success. Yet no door opened. Time would not turn about. Nothing he said when drugged made any sense. His babblings when beaten failed utterly to come true; far from enhancing his reputation, they faded away like so much smoke. Until at last Yeremoth and Shaham consulted and gave the order to desist. It would come when it was ready.

The elders turned their eyes from him and went their way. The small band of men scattered too.

Although the morning was still young, Hivai felt a leaden roof of fatigue descend on him. Slowly he walked along the wall, crossed the culvert that ran out of the city, and continued on his way. The wall looked different. Many men stood on it, shading their eyes to peer out into the distance. The enemy was not to be seen.

Large and lanky, he ambled on toward the pool. The marketplace was changed too. Three or four groups of strangers sat between its stalls with their belongings, breaking bread with their children. Refugees from some outlying farm, he thought, wondering wearily who had let them in. Perhaps they had tricked the guards, or stolen in with their flocks, tying themselves under the rams' bellies. Who could know? With the insolence of despair, they had spread their faded mats and sat down to eat, installing themselves, confident that no one would drive them away. The idol vendors in the marketplace glanced covetously at them and their bundles. As Hivai passed by, one of their children reached out and grasped his foot, smiling up at him from the damp pavement, his cheeks bronzed like a pomegranate. Hivai kicked free, and the child let out a solitary whimper. Yeremoth will have them killed, he thought. The idol vendors did not budge.

Annoyed at himself, he kept walking, as if to inspect, or protect, the city. Its weakest point was in the north. Here the houses were few, and the slope beneath them fell away in a thicket of bushes and nettles that were dusty-dry from the summer. Fig trees sprawled over the rocks. The winter had been rainy, and the harvest was abundant. Hivai followed a narrow path that led to the northern wall, treading on the rank caper plants that grew out of an abandoned stone fence. Swarms of bees reveled round him like wedding guests.

He spat the last dust from his mouth. The figs will whore too, he thought moodily: strangers will pick them and eat them while our corpses litter the rocks. Gibeon suddenly seemed wide open, insubstantial, an illusion more than a city: a man need only lean against its wall, or shout aloud, or sound a ram's horn, and everything would come tumbling down. Would that his arms were walls.

The jug in front of Bagbag's house was turned upside-down, signifying a visitor. He hadn't meant to visit her, yet after striding on a bit over ground strewn with rotten figs, broken pottery, and garbage, he changed his mind. He would go see her and chase away the whelp inside, he thought, finally finding an object for his anger. He would take him by the scruff of his neck and toss him out.

But when he stooped to let his tall frame through the low doorway, the visitor was already carefully adjusting his cloak and belt. Hivai did not know the man, a stranger who made himself so inconspicuous that he was all but invisible, unlike the local Canaanite dogs, who hadn't the least notion of manners. Without favoring him with a glance, Hivai strode into the small room, filling it with his bulk while his eyes grew accustomed to the darkness.

Two narrow windows let in a bit of light, which fell in patches on a worn purple rug. A small tallow candle in a wall niche was doubled by its reflection in a coaster of hammered copper. Old, tired, and rheumy-eyed, Bagbag sat on a pile of ancient rugs and scraps of wool, trying to clean up some honey that had spilled from a broken jar on the floor. Before Hivai could sit, she seized him by his cloak, gripping it tightly. What should a man do that he might live? Tell me, Hivai. What.

She burst into tears when he asked her what the matter was, agitatedly wiping her nose, from one nostril of which hung a large ring. They'll slit our throats, she wailed. We'll be butchered like sheep on a feast day. I tried to read the honey and saw blood.

He railed at her foolishness. The strength of his anger frightened her into ceasing her sobs. Blinded by tears, she collapsed on her knees before him by the piles of rugs, hands webbed with the golden honey that also stuck to her sleeves. She rooted for his private parts like an infant seeking the breast, murmuring as she fumbled for them, what will become of us, Hivai, tell me what. You're a prophet, surely you know.

So she too expected him to prophesy, he thought. Was there anyone left in Gibeon who did not clutch at his cloak?

Bagbag kept talking quickly, her hands busy. Ben-Nerbaal had been to see her that morning, she said. Ben-Nerbaal had told her to go to Ai. Ben-Nerbaal had said that Ai was stronger than Gibeon.

If that's what Ben-Nerbaal told you, he said crossly, why don't you go there? His seed spurted out quickly, without pleasure.

Should I? She lifted to him eyes full of sly hope. Should I go to Ai, O prophet?

He tore himself away from her kneading, honeyed hands, threw her a coin, and strode back out into the sunlight. Four or five of the clowning children were waiting outside, eyes painted and cheeks rouged just like Bagbag's, hands mimicking hers to his face. Did she milk some prophecy from you, Hivai? piped one of them as he passed.

He didn't look at them. Turning, he walked back into the city, to be met again by the loud buzzing of the flies that had gone on annoyingly all morning, and by the fractured bleating of the sheep, each time coming from somewhere else, though at this hour they shouldn't have been heard in the city at all.

All that day, and the next day too, the city was not as it had been. The Gibeonites were helpless, diminished; small groups of them huddled together, hands raised contentiously, imploringly. The circles they walked in kept shrinking, as if the siege were already upon them, within the walls, in the streets, in every house. One mustn't stray too far. It was dangerous. They stuck close to the city wall. Their speech lessened too.

Every now and then some young boy came dashing from the wall, shouting they're coming, they're coming, until his wild laughter and that of his friends, scampering away for dear life, informed the townsmen that once again they had been made the butt of a joke. Angry men ran after the boys to thrash them. The boys escaped every time.

The enemy was not to be seen. Nothing stirred in the bushes on the mountains; no campfires flickered there at night. Only the cattle egrets still sailed low above the valley, looking for the missing cows. Four army veterans stood before a house, rubbing old shields with tallow and passing the rust-eaten head of a spear through a fire. Half of the men watching them claimed that the fire was too hot, and half that it was not hot enough. The odor of rust mingled with the smell of tallow already rancid from the sun. Nearby an elderly man looked on, telling old war stories. At first the others listened; then they spat. The fellow was baking stones for supper, grinding water at the mill. There hadn't been a war in Gibeon since the days of their great-grandfathers.

The days went by. No one went out to the fields, neither the women to gather kindling nor the men to tend the crops and trees. On Yeremoth's orders the gate was kept shut. Gangs of men roamed the city, accosting the women; yet their hearts were not in it, they simply went through the motions, a single sharp word sent them flying. Here and there down some street, beneath a leafy carob or fig tree, groups of idlers sat playing bones, their laughter sudden and harsh. The clowning children were everywhere, marching up and down the steps like ludicrous squads of soldiers with swords made of hawthorn branches, until the elders chased them off with curses that rattled like lethal stones down the sloping streets. People complained that the summer was the hottest ever, hot and oppressive without end. Only the women still went about their business, bent silently over their housework, hiding their fear, which grew from day to day in a great silence.

The enemy was not to be seen. Once or twice some of the more daring shepherds took their flocks out to pasture beneath the city wall, less than a stone's throw away from it, struggling to keep their balance on the steep slope; but the guards quickly drove them back in. Those are Yeremoth's orders. Why don't you ask Yeremoth, perhaps he will not refuse you. The shepherds stood there timidly, shuffling their feet, not a word in their dry mouths. They were afraid to ask Yeremoth. Back in the city with their flocks, they went to bed at high noon, pulling their heavy cloaks up over their heads to shut everything out.

Little by little the goods disappeared from the marketplace. At first the burdenless porters still hung around, empty-handed and straight-backed as they had not been for years, regarding each other with slow wonder. There had never been time for it before. Unused to such idleness in the middle of the day, they stood waiting for something to happen. The days were marked by small panics, each shout causing fright, each donkey's bray making them jump, until the tension was dispelled by embarrassed laughter. Yet though they mocked one another's fears, all were afraid. Those with anything worth stealing hid it in their houses, in their storerooms, in their cellars, or else cached it in the rocky ground at night, covering the spot with large stones. Women wrapped their jewelry and buried it when no one was looking, hurriedly sticking a branch in the freshly dug earth to make it look like a new sapling. Little was bought, little sold. The stalls of the idol vendors were deserted, their business gone from the edges of the pool: no graven images were left for sale, not even gold. The men stood in the empty marketplace in groups, uncertain what they were doing there. Then they stopped coming. The market is dead, they said. The sun alone still filled its empty spaces, baring the cracks in its grooved paving stones and their streaks of grime.

The days went by. One day some men announced that they were going out to the fields beyond the wall to bring back grain and fruit. They left in the middle of the night and never returned. In the morning the bodies of two guards were found by the gate, run through by daggers. Large flies were already swarming over their rigid jaws. Yeremoth came to the gate in person, looked at his slaughtered men, and walked angrily away. Yeremoth will catch the murderers, it was said in the city. He will skin them alive.

But the departed men's households brazened it out. Their sons, they claimed, had gone to meet the enemy far from the city; they had taken the war to the enemy and would fight to save Gibeon and its inhabitants. More and more people began to spread this story. In one family's house a spit was set up, a calf slaughtered, and meat handed out in the street. The town cheered its heroes and brought their families gifts: honey, branches of sycamore, packets of myrtle, coins, little blue stones brought by the Philistines from the south. The hands of the proud fathers were kissed for the merit of having a savior of the city for a son. Behind their backs, people laughed and winked. They knew the departed men had gone to Ai. Ai was strong. The only necks they had saved were their own.

Now the guards were afraid to man the gate at night. Halfway through the first shift they slipped away to their homes, where they burrowed into their cloaks, blankets, and quilts and slept until the stars grew pale. Slaves and hirelings were stationed in their place. Since no one walked the streets at night for fear of the enemy, the subterfuge went unnoticed. Those who lived near the gate could hear the sounds of reveling until dawn, of drunken voices and bleating women echoing among the large stones.

The days went by. The sun grew milder; there were more and more clouds, their heavy shadows moving upon the mountains like legions on the march. Summer ended quickly, as if cached away too. Longingly they watched the fruit in the valley rot on the trees, dropping to be eaten by great clouds of raucous birds that arrived with the eastward-racing clouds in the sky, wave beneath rippling wave, rising, falling, swirling in endless circles. Flocks of incessantly crying starlings invaded the city, swarming over trees, rooftops, hedges, and ridgepoles until driven off with clubs and much banging of pots and pans. With the autumn breeze came the smell of rotted grapes, as heady as wine, and the fierce, sweet, cloying odor of ripe figs. Summer was over. The city was barricaded tight.

People complained day and night and learned to live with their complaints. No one rebelled. The millstones continued to grind. Large jars of olive oil stood against the walls and all the storerooms were full of lentils and beans. And yet people stared at the full jars and sacks as if looking right through them. There will be hunger, they said; it isn't far off. Sometimes they stole a glance at Hivai as he passed. Perhaps he had some prophecy at last. Perhaps he knew what no one else in Gibeon could know.

No prophecy came. Day and night he tormented himself, tossing sleeplessly in bed, wringing his hands, wishing he were dead. Nothing happened. When he walked in the street, he looked straight ahead and ignored all greetings, seeing no one, stopping for no one, letting no one ask him any questions. They stared at him reproachfully, as if he and he alone should be the one to know.

Autumn brought contention. Cut off from their pasture, the herds, having eaten all the fodder in the storerooms, began raiding the gardens by the houses, gobbling bean and chick-pea and celery and the soapwort planted by the housewives between hedges. The black goats were the worst, devouring not only fruits and greens but the very bark off the trees, which they stripped with an unstoppable hunger. The whole city became one great hunger of goats. Thatch roofs vanished from the low houses, leaving their occupants shivering at night; whole rows of vegetables suddenly disappeared as if the autumn wind had swept them away; onions were rooted from the ground, whether by hoof of beast or secret hand, no one knew.

Anger stalked the houses. A woman seized a sharp spike and killed her neighbor's cow for eating her squashes. A man brutally thrashed his own brother for stealing broad beans from the man's wife. Soon the whole city will be a desert, cried the women. Soon it will be a wilderness. Come see the mighty citadel of Gibeon turn into a land of jackals. They looked for Shaham to judge them, but Shaham was not to be found. No one knew where he was. Some said he had gone to Michmash. Some said to Azekah. Perhaps he would return soon.

Every day at noontime the novice priests paraded out of the temple, flagellating themselves with stone-tipped, brass-studded whips until they bled. Singing in low voices to the rhythm of the lashes, they went from street to street, regarded in silence from the doorways, they and their ominous chant: one-and-two, one-and-two. Skin flayed on half-naked bodies, they would swoop down without warning on one of the houses, from which came a heaven-rending cry. Often a man ran after them into the

street, tearing his hair and pleading with them to take his son if
they must, but to leave him his fattened calf. Begetting sons was
easy, but what prophet, priest, or elder could replace a prize
calf? . . . Yet the priests never gave back their prey. Nor did they
stop chanting. Thin and agile, their whips thwacking one-and-
two on their brightly oiled skin, they marched back to the temple, leaving only their brusque laughter behind them.

Stench began to spread too. At first dead dogs and poultry
were thrown over the wall, decomposing where they lay. One
morning, however, a woman died in childbirth and a man of old
age. Gibeon was built on outcrops of solid rock, lumps of hard-
ened gray with hardly any earth on them. Afraid to bury the
dead outside the wall, they kept the corpses at home. No one
knew what to do with them. The hired keeners sat by the virgin sycamore, not knowing when to begin or end their dirge.
No one bothered to dismiss them. A great unease descended on
the city whose dead lay waiting at home. All night the voices of
the keeners were heard in the sleepless town. The crying of children awakened the dogs, and the howls of dogs awakened the
donkeys and cows, each renewed outburst taking a long while
to subside.

One day Hivai went looking for Shaham, striding forcefully
as if squashing something with each step, his cloak over his nose
to shut out the stench. If Shaham had gone to Michmash, he
thought, then from Michmash he would bring him back. He
would bring him back from the mountains of Lebanon if he had
to, by the scruff of his neck, and sit him down and make him
judge the people.

Fists clenched, he stormed into Shaham's house adjoining the
wall, almost kicking in the door. Two or three women fled
quickly to the attic, veiling themselves with their shawls. He was
about to follow them when some plaits of dried garlic stirred
beneath the wattle ceiling, and Shaham emerged from behind

them. His beard was unkempt, he wore a coat to keep warm, and in his right hand he held a smoking censer, which he swung back and forth against the malodor as the Gibeonites had learned to do. He did not bother to greet his visitor, but simply stood, flapping his arms with great anger like a demented bird. Of course there was no justice in the city. How could justice be dispensed when the enemy was at the gate? How could there be slave or master or man of might before the law, when tomorrow the enemy might come and make masters of the slaves? If it was true, as Hivai said, that the people were killing each other for a handful of chick-peas, then this too was from the gods, and he, Shaham, was blameless. If Hivai wanted justice so badly, he could judge the people himself. He, Shaham, was not leaving his house. Unless, that is, he went to Ai. Ai was stronger than Gibeon; tonight, indeed, if there was still any respect for an elder in the city, he would order the gate opened and depart. And if Hivai said another word about justice, he might reflect on the fact that not only justice was missing in Gibeon but prophecy too. Let him go to the marketplace and prophesy instead of wasting his time. Let him prophesy to the wind, or to the tree, or to anything he wished. Let the people know what a man should do that he might live.

No prophecy came.

Hivai's family, too, looked at him expectantly. So did the neighbors. So did the man who had paid a bride price for his son, now trapped within the walls of the city, unable to bring his bride home. So did he who had bought a field and he who had given a loan against the wool of the lender's sheep. It did no good to lock the door against them; their silent beseechings assailed him through the walls. You're a prophet, Hivai. Tell the people, that they may know.

That evening, unable to bear the muteness of the heavens any longer, Hivai seized a small slave child with his left hand, carved out his bowels with his right hand, and dumped the steaming mess in the street to scrutinize. Through the gaseous fumes he clearly made out the crenellated walls of Ai.

A surge of wild joy gripped the city. Some men ran quickly and fell upon the refugees camped by the pool, whose sudden screams were quickly silenced; in their bowels, too, a city was sighted, stone piled heavenward on stone. Ai, it could only be Ai.

All Gibeon seemed to be outdoors. Here and there little fires of thornbushes burned between the houses, making the whole city flicker, casting light and shadow on people by turn. Eagerly, almost with relish, they described the stabbing of the Philistine fishmonger who had been stranded in the city since the locking of the gate. He had had a woman in Gibeon, whom he visited each time he came with his fish-laden donkey, and it was in her house that his murderers had found him. The man was hairy, with a chest like a fur coat, out of which the blood spurted as though from a spring ringed by creepers. In vain had the woman tried to staunch his blood with rags before running outside so that she would not see his death. Other men, it was said, had attacked the home of the Canaanite fortune-teller, killing her and looting her household gods, each leaving with a figurine beneath his cloak. Tomorrow, joked the Gibeonites, the idol vendors would do a brisk trade. The marketplace would come to life again.

A band of rouged and painted children, their lips very red, their wide eyes lined with antimony, went with the killers to show them other houses. There, over there, that's the house of the hired hand from Azekah. The wife of the man who lives here comes from Ramah. That's the place of the slave from Beth-Horon.

The man from Azekah was found in the wool fuller's house, which was burned to the ground with him in it. The acrid stink of charred felt and wool hung all night above the city, mingling with fetor from the temple. The wool fuller went along with the mob, his mouth agape as he watched all he owned go up in flames. He did not protest.

Standing in the dark streets, their faces aflicker, the others gave their assent. Dry-mouthed, they declared that the killers had done well to dispatch the foreigners. They had brought the evil eye on the city and its inhabitants; they had sucked its lifeblood like so many leeches, eating its food and drinking its water. Let the enemy appear at the gate and they would join him at once.

Thornbushes crackled in the flames. Slowly, their nostrils tickled by the smoke, the Gibeonites inhaled the good, familiar smell, and felt reborn. All summer long they had been utterly worthless; sluggardly, silent, ineffectual. Now autumn had come, and with it fire and night. Now was the time to show no mercy to those who deserved none and to remove the curse from the city. Now was the time to be Gibeonites. They were their old selves again, once more they felt that they were men. The whole city talked of nothing else.

Hivai entered his home and called for his daughter Sahali. It was already two years—from her twelfth birthday—since she had replaced her mother in his bed. Her thin, sun-bronzed, extravagantly bejewelled hands with their acornlike thumbs drove his body wild. He even liked it when she sobbed, liked it better than the way his other women lay beneath him as patient as cattle.

Once Sahali's mother had approached him, openly obsequious. Might she be struck down by lightning if she did anything to anger her lord, whose slightest aggravation she wasn't worth; yet since the day he had graciously honored Sahali by elevating her to his bed, she had gone around like a queen with her anklets, bangles, and rings, lording it over her mother and sisters. She refused to do the least bit of housework; might her mother, Hivai's maidservant, hope to die if it weren't true.

Hivai listened in silence. Then he beat Sahali, though not

hard enough to spoil her looks. He beat her mother, too, to teach her not to bear tales. Sahali laundered, spun, and fetched water as before, a sickly shadow of what she had been.

Now she came, jangling her anklets and chewing on an almond, her many braids dripping oil. Listlessly, without removing the almond from her mouth, she undid her dress. He looked at her sharply: she was as lifeless as a shepherd's fire that has been rained on all winter.

He asked if she too was afraid of the approaching invaders. She nodded.

Then and there he made up his mind. Had he himself not seen Ai in the bowels of the child?

He told her to saddle up the donkey, take two of the servant boys, and set out with them for Ai. And to be sure to keep her face veiled, so that no one in the city would recognize her.

Redoing her dress, she was gone with a bound, as if suddenly resurrected. He understood her haste only too well. But though it was like a stab in the heart, he did not change his mind.

That night he wrapped himself in a large sheepskin coat and went to walk them to the gate. In the house Sahali's mother was wailing, gouging her cheeks and tearing her hair so as not to be accused of rejoicing in her daughter's departure. At the door she kissed her again and again, throwing herself on the doorstep and tearfully seizing the girl by the ankles until Hivai kicked her roughly and ordered her back inside.

It was very dark. The sky was overcast. The donkey's hoofs pattered on the stones like thin rain. One of the servant boys glanced at the sky and predicted rain soon. No one answered.

The hired guards at the gate recognized Hivai at once. Servilely, they hurried to open the stile for him. The dark square with its stone walls as high as the sides of a well were strewn with empty jugs and rags that stank of vomit. The three cloaked figures and the donkey descended the steep slope without looking back. Once the donkey slipped on a wet rock, but one of the boys caught it and helped it laboriously back to its feet. No doubt Sahali had loaded it with more than she had been told she might take.

They vanished in the mist and Hivai turned and walked back. The rain beat down harder. He let the large drops run down his face without wiping them away.

It rained for days and days, and even when it stopped the rain echoed on, dripping from every tree and clump of reeds to trickle through the silent night. The Gibeonites retreated indoors. Many brought in their livestock from their pens, huddling by their sides to keep warm. Mornings, when the fog lifted, the wet boulders shone so whitely in the light that there was no telling where they ended and the clouds began. The low winter sky seemed to have trapped the light between it and the earth in a single pale, horizontal plane. The bad smell was diluted; at times it was possible to breathe pure air. Here and there it was said that the enemy might not come at all, that perhaps the curse had been removed from the city when all the foreigners were killed. It was they who had put an evil spell on Gibeon. Perhaps the enemy had struck out for another city, and they could soon go back to their old ways. Tomorrow or the day after, people said, the gates would be opened again. They slept better too.

Not for long, though. One morning the lookout came running from the tower to shout excitedly, almost incoherently, that it was upon them: a band of men was coming up the road from Beth-Horon, in no time they would be upon the city.

Quickly men climbed the wall to see the enemy. But it was not the enemy at all. There was no glint of armor, no flash of spear in the sunlight that pierced the dark clouds. Little by little the arrivals could be made out more clearly. There were about twenty of them, tired and miserable, barely limping along as if they had been on the road for many days. Two of the youngest reached the gate first. Imploringly, they looked up at it, beards angled toward the sky. They were, they said, from Ai. The invader had put the city to the sword. Of all its men, women, and livestock, only they had escaped with their lives. Would that the sons of Gibeon might open the gate and give them a place to rest their heads. Were not the Gibeonites brothers? Then let them be saviors, too.

Yeremoth, tense and loud, ordered the gate kept shut. Then he went out to the newcomers through the stile, clambering quickly over the rocks. Keeping his distance, he let no one clutch the hem of his cloak, or slip a pleading hand through his belt, or make any claim on his hospitality. From the high rock on which he stood he announced in a stentorian voice that there was no food or water in Gibeon. Let the refugees from Ai go where they wished; let those meant to live, live, and those meant to die, die, and Gibeon be free of blame. He turned back toward the city, a mighty figure, oblivious of the desperate cries for help. The guards made sure to lock the stile well behind him.

For several days the refugees remained on the plateau beneath the wall, begging to be taken in. Some of them were obviously sick, lying slack-jawed on the wet rocks, their gaze averted from the city as if it were not there. Their wretchedness was all that spoke for them. The Gibeonites stood on the wall, looking down on them without a word.

Then the survivors from Ai collected their bundles, helped the sick to their feet, lifted their small children to their shoulders, and straggled off toward Beth-Horon. The plateau before the city was deserted again. Only the wind blew over the rocks, scattering bits of shrubs and bushes long uprooted from their native earth.

A few of the Gibeonites, as if frightened by their own fear, began telling one another in low voices that they did not believe Yeremoth. Indeed, had anyone gone with him outside the gate to make sure that the strangers were from Ai? Could the Aians be told by horns on their heads, or by having three hands instead of two? Ai was too strong to fall to any enemy. The refugees were not from there. Yeremoth had made it all up.

Most vociferous was a certain albino, who stood by the pool with tufts of bleached hair clinging to his neck, his face very red. All morning he told whoever cared to listen that Yeremoth had lied, that he had shamelessly sought to mislead them. He was a Canaanite dog, Yeremoth was, afraid that the Gibeonites would open the gate and desert the city for Ai. That was why, seeing a few last stragglers from the countryside, a ragtag and bobtail of goatherds and smithy's slaves, he had said they were refugees from there. Refugees from Ai, indeed! It was enough to make a person laugh. Ai's walls were as high as the heavens; they were standing to this day. The giant had yet to be born who could conquer Ai.

Gradually, people gathered around the albino, some moved by old grudges, others by anger, hatred, or fear. They stood violently bunched together, spitting at Yeremoth's name. The son of a dog was tricking them all. Not an inch had fallen of Ai, not one. The Gibeonites had slept so long with their cattle that they had become like cattle themselves, believing every lie Yeremoth told them. It was time to rise up as one man, to open the gate and go to Ai and be saved.

Yeremoth's guards dispersed them with clubs, but that still did not make them believe him. They could feel that the blows were not what they might have been, as if the clubs, too, were infected with doubt. Swollen with insolent triumph, the albino went home, a fawning retinue in his wake. The guards looked the other way.

Hivai believed. Ever since the refugees' arrival, his world had caved in on him. His head in his hands, he sat for long hours at home, his jaws working as if chewing the bitter taste of it: a false prophet. Suddenly, that was what he was. Not that it wasn't Ai he had seen in the bowels of the child. He had surely seen it; but he had misunderstood the portent. Such was the way of the little gods: they showed the supplicant enough of the truth to seduce him and played him for a fool. They mocked him, confounded him, just like the clowning children.

Yet he had withstood torture. He had withstood intoxication. The thick welts on his back were his witness. He had withstood everything but his own impatience. He had let himself be gulled like an ordinary fool, rushing to embrace a mirage with outstretched arms like a calf running to its mother's teats. What, after all, had the great gods wanted from him? Only that he wait, that he wait until he knew. But he could not wait. He had played them false, and now they had abandoned him forever.

He had seen Ai in the bowels of the child. With his own eyes he had seen it. But the prophecy had not been about the strength of Ai's walls. It had been about their weakness. Ai had fallen. The birds had pecked the flesh of Sahali.

Five old men walked in the val-
ley, bundles on their backs, their nostrils flared to inhale the
clean air and fresh scents. The rain had stopped overnight and
large patches of light drifted over the wet earth like windblown
fleece. Light poured through the tangled branches of an oak
tree, sparkled on the skeins of a spiderweb, cast its blinding
cloak on cassia and terebinth, reducing all colors to one. The
trees were silent after their flurried night. Twittering calls of
birds echoed everywhere. The scents in the air could not be
breathed enough of, as though with each breath a man added
years to his life. The sleek trees were the essence of freshness; the
very stones, washed of their film of dust, seemed to breathe.

It was beyond them why they had not thought of it before. At
first they bore themselves with dignity as city elders should; yet
no sooner were they out of the sight of the watchers on the wall
than their steps began to quicken. By the time they reached the
shepherds' well, they were almost running, slapping one another's backs and laughing uncontrollably. Out of breath, they
pushed aside the well stone with its cover of thorny branches and
drew the pure water, drinking and clamoring for more. They had
not drunk anything as good in many a month, for the pool in
Gibeon had long turned brackish, and it had not yet rained
enough to cleanse it.

They wet their heads and beards and splashed each other with water. At last, gasping, gurgling, soaking wet, and drunk with freshness, they sat themselves on the ground. Some last grapes and pomegranates hung from the branches, and they wolfed them down quickly, dripping juice on beards and sleeves. Ben-Nerbaal hung clusters of grapes on his ears and wagged his head slowly, while they all howled with laughter and called him Bagbag. Divlat shut his eyes and folded his hands on his belly like a pregnant woman. Each mind was crossed by the wistful thought that perhaps they need go no further. Perhaps they should stay right here, in this valley, until it was all over, siege, besiegers, and besieged.

Hivai sat off to the side, staring unseeing ahead. Since the arrival of the refugees from Ai, he had taken to blinking as if he were half-blind. Nothing was clear anymore. His secret was his jailer. If called by name, he didn't answer; if shaken, he awoke only partly from his trance. His mouth moved constantly, as if he were chewing.

The elders didn't even look his way. Only yesterday they had still been in Gibeon, their nostrils full of its stench, the brazen glances of the albino and his sycophants accompanying them everywhere. The clowning children had mimicked them mockingly, derisively. And though the taunts had died down each time Yeremoth's guards passed by with their big whips, the grumbling had never stopped. The elders knew well that if they did not take some action, not a stone of their houses would be left standing.

No one remembered whose idea it had been first. Until then the deliberations had been weary. No one knew what to advise, no one seemed to have a shred of wisdom left. It was Harsan who, furrowing his brow, remarked after a while that the invaders' god was born in the desert, whereas the gods of Gibeon were from the mountains. That was why he was a mystery to them. Perhaps he was related to the gods of Egypt.

They said nothing. There was nothing to say. The Egyptians, too, had come and gone. The mountains had conquered them also. Whatever did not turn into mountain itself was soon expelled.

Another while passed and Ben-Nerbaal pointed out that the god of the invaders was a youngster. That was what made him so strong. And the gods of Gibeon were old.

Morosely, they took their time to consider that. Ben-Nerbaal was right. Their own gods were old, they were no longer what they used to be. What had been gained by all the choice bulls and fat lambs and firstborn sons offered up to them? The gods of Gibeon had dined on the town's best beef and mutton and now they were not there when they were needed, they were past their prime, perhaps they were even dead. Or perhaps they had absconded like the swindling Philistine traders, whose tricks everyone knew. They took your money and in the morning they were gone, and with them the goods they had sold you—and what good was your hue and cry then?

At last Shaham spoke up. Slowly, clearing his throat as if from much cogitation, he declared: If their god is too young and brave to be defeated in battle, perhaps he is untutored enough to be fooled. Suppose we talked him into an alliance; would not Gibeon be saved?

They looked at him in amazement. Never in their lives had they heard anyone suggest that a strong god might be fooled. Petty trickery, of course, was something they knew all about. More than one Gibeonite kept his wealth buried in the earth to outwit the tax-man. At calving and lambing time, when the priests came to take the firstborn, they would hide the infant livestock in bushes and caves and pretend it had been a bad year. We must have sinned, they would tell the priests. The young have been carried off by plague. Perhaps we shall be better blessed next year.

Shaham's counsel, however, was of an entirely different nature.

It was beyond their capacity to understand. Or to believe in. Were they seriously expected to dupe the invaders' god by a ruse any shepherd lad could see through? Why, they would simply make a laughingstock of themselves. How small today was Shaham's wisdom, they exclaimed, how small and uninspired.

But Shaham, having spoken his mind, waited in triumphant silence, his beard pointing stiffly, his old eyes half-shut like a turtle's. No one could think of anything better. Gradually, as if getting used to a new dish that neither they nor their fathers had ever tasted, they began to accept what he had said. Each looked to the other for assurance. Perhaps it might work after all. Perhaps.

Only Harsan objected. We'll be their captives, he grumbled. Captivity, replied Shaham with a shake of his head, is a death you live to tell about.

Their spirits rose. All could feel how eager they were to set out. No man was wiser than Shaham, no counsel better than his. They would go forth from Gibeon to make sport of the invaders. The wisdom of Gibeon's elders would vanquish the boy-god and save the city. Yeremoth alone, it was decided, would remain behind with his guards, whose big whips would ensure law and order until their return.

Now, though, having set out, return was far from their minds. In the valley bathed in afternoon light, all such considerations appeared distant. Gone was the stench, which their clothes had shed only slowly, and with it the whole moldy, smelly, whining, noisy city, bleating dirges by night and rolling tangles of brawls from street to street by day. In the clean air and great silence they felt born anew. Their feet led them over the saddle of the almost bald ridge, where amid rocks nothing but a few cassia bushes and nettles grew. A welcome breeze blew and they walked bunched together, conversing. At the top of the ridge, Harsan climbed a bit further to get a better look. Shading his eyes, he looked in all directions before clambering back to join them. As far as the horizon, there was not a soul to be seen.

Slowly the sun sank westward, gilding the branches of the tall cypress trees scattered over the mountain. A flock of storks circled above them in the last light, rising back into the sky each time they touched the treetops, as if afraid to land. In the crystal-clear air, they could see very far. They stopped to take in the view, the worry lines smoothed from their faces as if by the first sunset of their lives. Hivai alone did not bother to look. Tall, but bent as though beneath a heavy burden, he trailed after them with his eyes lowered, seeing only the swiveling hips of the man ahead of him. He did not answer when spoken to, and after a while he was spoken to no more.

The autumn day faded suddenly. A cold wind blew from the west, cutting icily through the rags they wore. Unsure which direction to head in, they bunched more closely together and came to a halt.

With the cold came dejection, the melancholic blast of night. Though they were still near Gibeon, they felt far indeed from its candles and warm hearths. Who knew if they would return? There might be no way back. Or no Gibeon. Or no tomorrow.

Harsan signaled them to climb in his direction. Ascending a bit higher up the rocky slope, they came to a dry cave, its floor covered with dry old animal droppings. A carob tree hid the entrance, its branches so thick that the bushes beneath it had hardly been wetted by the rains. When the sun vanished and the world was gone for the day, they made a fire, laboring over its sparks as if breathing new life into themselves, fighting the fear that crept up the gnarled veins of their legs into their cold, bony knees, the knees of men who were old.

The fire was finally started. They sat around it warming their hands, then took some sprigs of chick-peas from their packs and roasted them in the coals. Smoke filled the chimneyless cave, and they lay coughing. Their talk was cut short by the darkness, which dispelled the closeness among them and turned each man in on himself.

Lying at a distance from the others, Hivai watched one or two of them rise and shake the fleas from his coat into the flames. They did not dare go far from the cave and urinated right outside it, stepping with a small, embarrassed laugh over the body of the prophet blocking the exit. After a while no one talked or stirred, and there was nothing but coughs, farts, snores, and a few last popping sounds of burrs exploding in the cinders.

It took Hivai a long time to fall asleep. Trapped by his secret, he was frightened even of sleep. He lived through the days in a fog, like a man wading through water, but the nights gripped him with terror. He feared the vengeance of the great gods as he had never feared anyone or anything in his life. Another day or two, another night, and it was sure to overtake him, hard and inevitable. He had no idea whether his death would be sudden, or if life would drain slowly out of him, ever so quietly, like the blood from slit veins, until sight faded, breathing ceased, heart beat for the last time. Had there been anyone to turn to, he would have turned. Had there been anyone to speak to, he would have spoken. But the great gods never showed themselves; they came and they went as they pleased. They knew he had sinned with the little gods. As did he. After such sin, there could be nothing.

He had lost track of the days. He could no longer recall when it had happened, when he had misread the portent of Ai, when the refugees had come and gone. He had been prepared to fall ill and die at once, but illness had scorned his large body. Now he followed the elders, planting foot ahead of broad foot, step after step after step. They were used to his silences. Out of one of them, perhaps, a prophecy would come at last. Wasn't that why they had taken him along? There was no way they could know that no prophecy was left in him, that he would never prophesy again. They slept, each man by himself, while he alone lay awake.

The skies clouded over again in the night and it began to rain once more, though thinly, with a stingy drizzle. The morning was cheerless. A thick fog covered the mountain, shutting out the world. The elders woke coughing in their cave. Listlessly, they ate the last of the good bread they had brought from Gibeon, casting the leftover crumbs in a corner and covering them with cold ashes. Now nothing was left but the stale bread dotted with mold, the bread of deceit. The cave smelled of mildew and human sleep. It was time to head eastward, toward the desert and the invaders. No one knew when they would encounter them. It could be in a day or in a month. Wrinkled, shivering, gray with morning, they packed their things.

They encountered them almost at once. They had just left the cave, Harsan having prodded Hivai to his feet with a kick, and were descending from the saddle of the ridge in an easterly direction, with fat Divlat bringing up the rear, when they were suddenly surrounded by a band of young men who seemed to have sprung from the bowels of the earth.

None of them heard their captors approach. They were thin and bronzed, a deep color of the sort that never fades, that belonged to the skin itself, more like a layer of desert sand than a suntan. They blinked a little, as if used to greater distances or flatter horizons, and they shivered from the cold. Several of them jumped from foot to foot to keep warm, like large grasshoppers. They were not at all like the local inhabitants.

Impatiently, unsmilingly, as though made rigorous by the morning cold, their captors assailed them with curt questions, one man interrupting another in a Canaanite that was hard to understand. Repeatedly, they inquired about the elders' city, as if guessing that Gibeon was nearby, barely a half-day's walk away.

The elders, however, pretended to know no Canaanite at all. Over and over they pointed to the north with a feigned show of patient rectitude. What city? There was no city. They came from far off, from the north, from the place of the great rivers and great gods. They were Hivites, not Canaanites. Had the Hebrew masters never heard of the Hivites? They were a great people living in the north of the world. They were only sojourning here in Canaan, they were not part of the local populace. No, not at all. They had come from afar with these bundles on their backs, all the provisions they had. Would the Hebrew masters care to see their bread that had gone bad and their worn-out shoes? Look how scratched their feet were—why, there wasn't a thorn or thistle in this whole accursed land that they hadn't stepped on. Who could believe that this bread that was dotted with mold had been still warm when they left home? The Hebrew masters could decide for themselves: would anyone choose to eat bread like this if he could get better?

They talked on and on, gesturing and holding up more proofs—a split waterskin, yet another torn shoe—until their captors finally understood. The young men stood around them, scratching their heads. They had no idea what to do with these unexpected prisoners, who came from no city, village, or even farm worth spying on, but were simply a band of old nomads speaking an incomprehensible tongue. They themselves had been sent ahead to reconnoiter; not a word had been said to them about taking captives, dead or alive.

In the end one of them convinced the others to take the prisoners with them. The elders breathed a sigh of relief. Harsan stealthily nudged Shaham in the ribs: surely the wisest of men, he! But though all had gone well so far, Shaham remained impassive. Crossly he gave the elders a heavy-lidded glance, as if signaling them to be still. The day was still young, and their fate had not yet been sealed. They had better save their breath for later.

All day long they followed their captors. The fog lifted all at once, like a heavy gray blanket raised from the valley, and a warm sun shone down on the world. The Hebrews walked very quickly. The elders could not keep up and fell behind, one of their thin guards circling back each time to berate them for not moving faster. They were being led on a long path that wound through the valleys, keeping their distance from the Jebusite farms visible here and there in the mountains to the south. Perhaps their captors were lost. Indeed, once or twice they re-crossed a valley they had already passed through before. They could have gone on in circles forever, round and round, never once climbing a hill to help them get their bearings.

When evening came the Gibeonites collapsed. They could not take one more step. Their breath came in quick gasps; their faces were crimson. It was all they could do to wipe the dusty sweat from their brows and suck the last of the water from their skins. Divlat, who had the most flesh on his bones, lay panting and half-dead.

But once the sun had gone down, the Hebrews were in no hurry either. They simply dropped to the ground, as if despairing of finding shelter for the night. Perhaps they didn't know how to look for it. They threw the elders some bread, which was hardly better than the moldy stuff brought from Gibeon, picked a few pomegranates, on which they sucked loudly, and fell asleep with few words, scattered all over the open field like abandoned belongings. Now and then, wild-haired and groggy with sleep, one of them stirred to drive away a jackal cub that kept approaching too closely, then lay down again like a dead man. It was past midnight when someone managed at last to crack the intruder in the teeth with a club. The animal yelped and vanished.

The Gibeonites huddled together. The moon came and went through tattered clouds, irregularly lighting shrewd old faces that laughed noiselessly into their beards. What fools their captors were. Why, they did not even know how to start a fire. Over and over they had mindlessly tried to kindle it with wet wood, like men who had no knowledge of winter. It was Harsan who had to gather dry twigs of burnet and find a fallen log, from the underside of which good chips could be hacked. It was Ben-Nerbaal who, that morning on the hillside, had to point out a shepherds' well that the Hebrews had passed without noticing. He had shown them how to roll aside the stone and how to draw the water. Why, they were like newborn babes in this mountain land, they and their god together.

They no longer feared the invaders. Their god was not of this country, neither bone of its bone nor flesh of its flesh. They knew they could prevail over him. Gibeon was mightier than any conqueror. With heads held high they would visit the Hebrew camp and speak with dignity; soon the Hebrew god would flee back to the desert he had come from and show his face no more in the land of men. And the invaders would flee with him, like chaff before the wind; from the desert they had come and to the desert they would return. No one would remember either them or their god. The mountain would remain, as always.

Hivai lay alone, as if none of this concerned him. What if the Hebrews came and what if the Hebrews went? The mountain would remain as always. And so would he and his sin. Until the great gods struck him dead.

He paid no attention to Divlat, who rose clutching his chest and groaning in the night, then lay down again and wheezed as if asking for something, perhaps water. For a moment he considered seeing what he wanted, but the thought failed to mobilize his body. Then Divlat's wheezing stopped, and Hivai fell into the sleep, as deep as a pit and as densely submerged as a death, that had overcome him each hour before dawn since the day of the refugees' arrival, a sleep both brief and unrestful.

In the morning Divlat was found dead. Harsan kicked him once or twice, turned him over on his back, and stood regarding him thoughtfully. Then he took out a dagger and cut off the dead man's right hand to present to their captors. The Hebrews looked at the bloody limb and did not know what to do with it. It was, Harsan explained, a token that the prisoner had died on the road, that he had not escaped or been sold into slavery. They were blameless for his death before their masters.

The Hebrews did not understand. At last one of them took the severed hand and flung it into the bushes, wiping his own hand with disgust. A large songbird took off from a bush in low, frightened flight and settled on another bush nearby. The elders looked at each other: had it been up to them, they would have gone to the first bush and searched there for eggs or fledglings. Their captors, however, did not even glance in its direction.

Again they headed eastward. The elders were silent, as if they had spent all their scorn the night before. Short, low clouds flew before the wind, fleeter than they were, as if the real march were taking place up there above the valley. Once, in a sudden, arrogant burst of speed, a Jebusite iron chariot overtook them. Drawn by a black horse, it raced past them from a dirt road on a hillside while they silently, obeisantly made way for it. The Jebusite, his head wrapped in a turban against the wind, cursed them and rode off, spattering mud in the faces of captor and captive alike.

Toward evening they heard many sounds of life, of livestock and camels and people. Around a bend in the road they came upon the Hebrew camp; composed of gray, badly weatherbeaten tents and some hastily constructed wattle huts, it sprawled over a large area. The elders stared at length, narrowing their eyes to slits through which the pupils hardly showed. Even ordinary robbers, even highwaymen, they thought, had finer dwellings than these. And the mindless way the tents were set up, at the very bottom of the valley! All that was needed was one good rain to wash the whole camp away.

A group of men and women came forth to greet the returning scouts, and soon all were part of one embracing, backslapping crowd. The elders tried to look the other way, letting the merriment blow past them.

They stood erect, straightening their cloaks in silence. Each knew what the others were thinking: like conquering heroes, that was how the scouts had been met. What had they conquered? Were they, the elders, such valuable booty that the whole camp turned out to cheer their captors? They stood without moving, as full of contempt as a jug is full of water. The slightest careless motion might send their derision spilling out.

They entered the camp. Their captors quickly vanished in the throng. No one showed the least interest in the four Gibeonites, who were left to fend for themselves.

Hivai, too, raised his eyes to look. The Hebrew camp had an air unlike any he had been in, and he did not know how to breathe it. All around was a great din, the commotion of evening. Children stepped fearlessly up to get a look at them. Tall, laughing women walked right by them with unveiled faces. They had no idea what was expected of them.

In the end they sat down beneath one of several mat awnings scattered haphazardly around the camp, whether tents or merely canopies one could not say. Some mud-caked reed mats lay beneath them for no apparent reason, and on these rested heaps of junk: broken-handled jugs, plucked sprigs of chick-peas, piles of earthenware jars, cabbages, dates, and black, strong-smelling goat wool. Nearby sat a bronzed young woman nursing a child.

Bare-faced and bare-breasted, she regarded them curiously, now and then wiping her nose with the corner of her dress. They turned insulted backs on her, contracting themselves with anger.

A second woman sat down by the first and began to converse with her. In her arms she held a small girl about four years old. The girl was crying quietly. From the corners of their eyes they could see a large, swollen abscess on her arm. Her mother collected some old sacks, seated herself upon them, made herself comfortable, and began to blow on the sore. Slowly she cooled it until the girl's crying grew softer and finally stopped altogether; yet still she went on blowing with a soft, soothing rhythm, while the elders shrugged their shoulders and narrowed their eyes still further, saying nothing.

Finally, a Hebrew came striding quickly up to them, and they rose. He was a short, stocky man with small hands that rose and fell in threshing movements as he spoke. If they would be so kind as to come with him, he said in the local language, he would take them to state their business before Ahilud. He spoke rapidly, with one swift glance at them, as if that were quite enough. As they followed him he rubbed his hands with satisfaction like a man whose affairs are going well. Their captors, he told them as they walked, had already informed the camp of their skills at hewing wood and drawing water. Perhaps, he smiled encouragingly, they would stay on in camp, because there was plenty of work for them.

They were brought to a tent in which about ten men were seated, any of whom could have been Ahilud. Once again they told their story: they were not from these parts, they were nomads, Hivites from the north, whose city was very far away; but they were skilled at all trades and would not deceive the Hebrew masters.

The men in the tent seemed uncertain. Frequently they

paused to consult among themselves, while the Gibeonites stood stiffly, waiting. In the end several long sentences were spoken to their stocky guide, who nodded and interpreted for them: the Hebrews would ask the judgment of Joshua, who was two or three days' march away. If the Gibeonites would be so kind as to remain in the meantime, not a hair of their heads would be harmed.

For two whole days they sat on the mat, waiting recumbent, chewing on a bunch of dried dates they had been given. They already knew that the camp was a small and lonely one, and they felt no fear. The air was free, without menace. Sounds of daily life came from everywhere: of cooking, of milking, of work tools, of children at play, and of women singing without hindrance. Even the mother of the girl with the abscess went on blowing on it day and night, as if she had no other work to do.

Thoroughly idle, they passed the time making fun of their captors. Did they think that their children were worth their weight in gold, had they bought them for pieces of silver? The Hebrew husbands must be worn out, their seed must be dry and infertile, for why else would they value each offspring of theirs as if it were an only child? And their wives—as insolent as black goats they were, a flock of goats got from the desert. What manner of men were these, their clothing more ragged than the Gibeonites' fraudulent tatters, leaderless, priestless, elderless? Why, the least slave in Gibeon was a more pleasing sight.

After two days the same stocky fellow came to them again. The camp, he said, was being struck. The messengers to Joshua had not yet returned, but Ahilud said they should proceed with the alliance, because there was no time to wait.

Quickly, without ceremony, they were brought back to the tent they had been in. A few men were seated inside, while four or five youths loitered by the entrance. Once again they were asked who they were and where they came from, and once again they swore they were Hivites from the north. Sojourners they were in Canaan, it was not their home.

The Hebrews barely appeared to be listening; other things were clearly on their minds. Stepping up to the elders, the youths knotted the corners of their cloaks into little foreskins, then did the same to the cloaks of the Hebrews. A man declaimed the words of the ritual in a strange language. Someone else fetched a dagger, tested it with a finger, and cut the knotted corners. The covenant was sealed.

Having unknotted their cloaks, the Gibeonites wished to say a few words, but the Hebrews rushed busily out of the tent, as if the whole matter no longer concerned them. The youths collected the cloth foreskins from the floor and handed several to the Gibeonites for a surety. They tucked the frayed strands of fabric in their belts, the tension draining from their old faces. It was done.

When Shaham, Ben-Nerbaal, and Harsan packed their bundles and set out to inform Gibeon that the siege was over, Hivai stayed behind. Harsan gave him a light kick. In another day or two, he warned, when the Hebrews find out they've been tricked, they'll have your hide. On your feet, fool! Let's go open the gates of the city.

But Hivai stayed where he was. He knew there was no man, beast, or bird in Gibeon that he ever wished to see again.

He attached himself to Ahilud's household.

At first he had no idea what his place was or what was expected of him. The Hebrews' customs were strange to him, as was their language; yet the rags he wore, the clothing of deceit, were much like their own dress, and no one paid him any attention. He wandered mutely about the camp, a tall, gangling figure full of humble willingness. When there was a burden to be carried, he carried it; when it was time to feed the few cattle, he fed them. From morning to night he was with the household, made happy by the least nod, gesture, or sign of understanding, which he returned with an exaggerated smile. Still afraid of being made to leave, he clung to the family as though they were his last refuge, sleeping on the edge of the mat, eating whenever anyone remembered to invite him to share the common pot. He never approached without being asked. At times he thought that if an enemy were to attack these people, he would defend them well with all his great strength; then they would love him, and he them. He knew that here and here alone the long arm of the great gods could never reach him.

As if accustomed to the desert, they could not stay long in one place. One morning, nobody knew why or when, they would rise bedraggled and quarrelsome, as if an ill wind had entered their gaunt bodies, dismantle the camp, and move with it to another hill, where once again they set up the same tents and booths. Call it restlessness. On each of these moves, they burdened him with much baggage, since he was a large man. He never complained. Nor did he ask why they kept changing hilltops.

When they discovered Gibeon's ruse, nobody asked for his hide. Perhaps they did not mind what had happened, or perhaps he was too strong and devoted to lose. Possibly they had even forgotten that he had ever come from Gibeon with the elders. He had become part of the landscape, a man like a tree of the field.

The first winter raged in, deluging the meager camp until there was not a dry spot left or a garment to keep a man warm. All they had was soaked through. Winds battered them day and night, without respite. They stayed in their dripping tents, venturing forth unhappily. Nearly everyone took sick. By now they knew that the valley was a bad place to camp when the torrents of water rushed down from the hills. They knew, too, how to look for shelter in caves and ledges in the hillside. Teeth chattering, trembling from cold, the desert tan grayed from their faces, they promised each other that when winter was done, they would settle down and build good houses.

The main Hebrew camp was far away, and they, sick and rheumy, made no great effort to catch up with it. Sometimes they sent out messengers, who did not always return. Perhaps the ways were impassable, or perhaps the messengers had fallen prey to marauders or to the wild animals that lurked in the dripping bushes. In time, no more were sent.

Hivai lay among them at night, as far from his old home in Gibeon as if there were no such place. A stone house was a thing of the past; so was a food cellar; so were tallow candles in their niches at night and the big-bellied wine and oil jars in their cool lofts. Here nothing came between him and the gray sky, or between his body and the unstable ground, over which, like earth-sweat, brown rivulets of mud flowed ceaselessly between the paths of the camp. Everyone was as caked with it as he was. No one bothered cleaning it off anymore. No one wore shoes anymore either, because they just weighed a person down. At night they sat around yawning wearily, scraping the mud off their soles, or from between their toes, with whatever implement, stick, or slaughtering knife they could get their hands on, bowed beneath the burden of winter. They talked little. They fell asleep at once.

Of Gibeon he never thought or dreamed. It was as though it were forbidden, a white-hot metal in his memory that would sear him if ever he touched it. Once or twice, dreaming that powerful strangers had come like bailiffs to take him back, he awoke with a cry. He apologized, wanting only to be unobtrusive, afraid to wake them with his troubled sounds. But they, too, often cried out loudly in their sleep.

One morning it snowed, the soft flakes falling like the plumage of doves. There was no sound. The livestock fell silent too, as if soothed by the white hand. The snow wrought a great peace. Frozen and amazed, they stepped out into the stillness, staring at the strange whiteness that had come to rest on tree, stone, and roof, and breathed the all-quiet, all-white air. Not a sound. Not an echo. The palm fronds covering the booths drooped forlornly. It was cold; but the sight of the white sky swirling soundlessly down kept them there for a long time. They tried catching the flakes. They stuck them in their mouths, surprised.

Toward evening the snow turned to hail and everyone ran to escape the fierce barrage. Only the children, fleeing their mothers' arms, danced gleefully about in it, knees red with frost. Their laughter filled the camp. On that white day, the world seemed to rest from all contention. Fear ceased, too. Until the hail ravaged the last of the snow and turned it to ugly little trickles of mud.

Slowly, gradually, Hivai learned their language, word by word, as if cutting it out of stone. His lips encircled the syllables, forming speech as if he were tasting it. Next, he started whispering the words to himself. Finally, in a low voice, he began to speak.

He never alluded to Gibeon. He had excised his former life as though it had never been. He knew very well that the ways of Gibeon would not find favor in these people's eyes. Nor was there any way to explain them. Gibeon was different.

They never inquired about it either. Only once did Marit, Ahilud's wife, ask him what he had been there before settling among them. She asked in a loud, critical voice, a frown on her face. She had suspected him since the day of his arrival, whispering at night to Ahilud that he was a spy, Hivai was, and not to be trusted. A spy: one day they would all see that she was right. Now she stood facing him, a wide-hipped woman almost as tall as he was, asking in severe tones. Hesitantly he replied that in Gibeon he had been a prophet.

Marit would not take that for an answer. What, she wanted to know, had he prophesied there?

Though he knew he should not tell her, he did not know how to refuse. Perhaps he was unaccustomed to being questioned by a woman. As sparingly as he could, he told her about his vision of the drought, about prophesying the great plague, about knowing in advance that Yeremoth's father would die.

Marit frowned harder, thought a moment, and declared that this was a seer, not a prophet. How so? he asked offendedly.

A prophet, she replied, was a man like Moses, who gave the Law and led the people in the desert. If Hivai had given Gibeon no law, he was neither a prophet nor the son of one, but only a seer. And with that she was off, not waiting for a reply.

It enraged him.

A day or two later, while cutting wood with Ahilud, he inquired discreetly about the Law given by Moses. Was it a secret matter, or could it be discussed? Ahilud seemed perplexed. It

was a question, he replied, that had to be asked of those wiser
or older than he. He himself had been but a boy when the Law
was given in the desert. He had never studied it much. He knew
that it forbade a man to murder or to bear false witness. Truly,
he did not know much more than that, but everyone knew that
the Law was very good.

Hivai humbly begged to be forgiven for his ignorance; but if it
was not too much to ask of his lord Ahilud, when was a man forbidden to murder? One could not murder an elder or kill a priest
in broad daylight in Gibeon either. Surely, a man would not murder his maternal uncle; in Gibeon, too, it was a transgression.

No, said Ahilud. A man must never murder anyone. That was
the law. He could not tell Hivai any more.

Hivai was confused. It was too much for him. He did not ask
again.

One way or another, the winter was coming to an end. The
constant rush of water that they heard day and night had
stopped. Looking eastward across the valley of the Jordan, it was
possible to see the mountains on the other side again, a deep
mauve in the sunset. The constant mud was hardening back into
earth. Flowers covered the hillsides, red and purple and deep
pink; the inner force of the earth burst out, parading its powers
in a festive array on slope and bluff. In the Jebusite farms across
the valley, men were seen going out to the fields to work the
land.

They had no land. Here and there they had carved out tiny
plots, scarcely bigger than a man's hand, that they managed to
fence off and work: a piece of earth between olive and mastic
tree, a few square feet in the valley, or clinging to the side of the
hill. They took what they could find: abandoned strips re-
claimed by the kingdom of weeds, slopes so steep they could be
stood on only by grasping a tree, soil strewn with rocks and
stones that no one else on earth would have farmed. They rooted

themselves in the mountain as if they were plants themselves, as if a desert wind had sown them by accident and left them to spring up among the boulders, sprouting wherever there was a handful of earth. They learned to leap across the rocks like the goats by their sides, to find their footing in places where even donkeys slipped and fell. They gathered rocks and stones to fashion terraces, leveling the earth with bare hands to keep it from washing away. And there they planted.

Those who found land in the valley below were no better off. Their small yield was soon stolen, whether by the nomadic marauders who cast terror on the countryside, or the Canaanites, or the Jebusites from the mountains. The Jebusites would wait patiently for a crop to ripen, passing it for months as if it were not there, while measuring it with a sideways glance, sure of possession in the end. No sooner had the reaper begun his harvest than they swooped down and made off with it all, leaving behind trampled stubble, broken branches, and tears. There was nothing to do about the Jebusites. They had chariots of iron.

There was much contention in camp. Some said it was foolish to work the land. They were a people of shepherds, and shepherds they would always be, wandering untrammeled from place to place with their flocks. What was the sense in planting trees for others to eat their fruit, or sowing crops for the Jebusite to plunder? Shepherds they were and shepherds they should remain. Their birthplace was the desert, stone houses were not for them; they and their children were meant for mats and booths, free to come and go as they pleased.

Others were silent, as stubborn as the earth itself.

No decision was ever made to stay or move on, yet each year there were more of those who answered with silence. Perhaps it was the winter that helped make up minds, perhaps the children born in the camp, trembling from the wet and the cold and bleating like baby lambs not long for this world.

They had not the strength to live like that, but also none to decide. Each winter, the first and the second and the third, they told themselves that come spring they would build houses. But they never did. They could not make up their minds. It was not until the fourth year that one or two men gathered large stones and constructed a shelter of them, a rough, solid booth that was not divided into rooms. Others piled stones in a corner and looked at them all summer without building, until once again the winter rains arrived.

Gradually, in the fifth year, stone shelters began to go up. And yet, the Hebrews reassured one another, these were really more tents than houses. They could still come and go as they pleased; they had simply built roofs to keep their children warm and dry.

When spring came, however, they went nowhere. Nor was there anywhere to go. No longer did they live by their flocks alone, but rather grew bread from the earth, glancing up at the sky to see what the prospects for rain were. Backs bent, their vertebrae showed through the dark skin beneath their rags like sharp beads. Calluses covered their hands. They had become one with the mountain, they and their crude dwellings, like vegetation that had pushed up out of the desert and slightly changed the face of the hills. That was all. Yet when sometimes, hot and fierce, a desert wind blew through the camp, they would stand for a moment gazing silently eastward, breathing the wind in deeply, with endless longing.

They themselves could not say when the camp began to have a name. It was no longer just Ahilud's house, or Shirah's house, or Gomer's house, here today and gone tomorrow. From now on the houses on the hill were called Aner, and those in the valley, Eter. No one invented these names. They sprang up by themselves and quickly spread throughout the camp. Perhaps they grew out of the mountain. Suddenly they were there.

White cattle egrets came, too. They walked fearlessly behind

the cows, as if they had always been there. And after them arrived an itinerant peddler who, much to the joy of the women,
included the camp in his rounds. At harvest time Ahilud's
daughters returned from the fields with rings in their ears, their
bodies singing. From the hayloft at night came the sound of
flutes and the voices of lads and maidens in song.

Hivai did not build a house. He lived in a wattle hut at one
end of the land and never visited Ahilud's home. Nor did the
family, once it had built a stone house of its own, invite him to
eat with them anymore. One of the youngsters would bring him
out a pot or a large stack of flat, round bread, or else he himself would make a fire and toast the grain he had been allowed
to gather. Sometimes, too, Ahilud generously made him a gift
of some roast meat or a pinch of dough, or else rewarded him
with a coin or some new wool from the shearing. His needs
were few.

Marit despised him. Just look at the prophet, she would say,
narrowing her eyes. Before you know he'll be prophesying
about us, and you can be sure it won't be anything good. Be still,
be still, said Ahilud loudly, but she would not be.

Ahilud's sons, though, had no qualms about visiting Hivai.
They would come bringing a shoe to be cobbled, a wooden
plowshare to be sharpened, a plant to ask if it could be eaten.
He had a reputation for being a good workman. Once he even
took some reeds they had brought and made them some fine
flutes. They thanked him with a rough pat on the shoulder and
forgot him the moment they left him, as though he himself were
but another of their tools.

He was not at peace. When the day's work was done and it
was time to go home, they to their house and he to his hut, the
thoughts came thick and fast. He had worked for them for seven
years, which now seemed like one long, laborious day. Not once
had he failed them, not for a moment had he left the camp or

stopped cutting wood, fetching water, and faithfully doing his chores. And yet he was still as much an outsider as ever, unversed in their Law, walking the same straight line every day from the fields to his hut and from his hut to the fields. True, their god had kept his word: as long as Hivai lived in their midst, he was protected. The great gods had not come to wreak vengeance. He was alive and well. The god of the Hebrews dealt honestly and had neither cheated nor betrayed him. Yet neither had he revealed himself. Though Hivai would gladly have brought him a thanks-offering, the god had eluded him.

He thought and he thought, and the more he thought the bitterer it made him. He could feel his gorge rise. Was he a leper or a woman in her menses that he should not be allowed to worship their god with them? He had served them faithfully, and they had let him down. Never once had he seen their god. Was he big or small? Did he speak with a man's voice or a woman's? They had built houses, too, and hidden the sacrifice, as if he were unworthy of seeing it. They had even told him there was none, which was nothing but a mealymouthed lie. Could a house be built without blood being spilled and a victim laid under the cornerstone? He was not a gullible child. They were keeping things from him, they were leading him astray and not letting him pay his debts to their god. Against his will they had made him an ingrate and a stranger.

His sense of injustice grew from day to day. He was a prophet, not a slave, and he would see their god. He would bow down to him and prophesy in his name, faithfully, as he had done long ago, and all the Hebrews would listen. They alone stood between him and their god, as if he were a dark secret. But he would find him; he would study the Law, and regain his old powers, and prophesy. They and they alone kept him from his true vocation.

One day in the field he asked Ahilud, but he couldn't get a straight answer. Their God, said Ahilud, had no form or body or shape. No man could see him and live, except perhaps Moses. That was the truth of it, even if he, Ahilud, did not entirely understand. But he was the same God who had taken them out of the land of Egypt, and given the earth to men, and given a Law upon the earth, for which he held them accountable.

Hivai persisted. But if your god has no body, he asked, how did he smite all the other gods? To which Ahilud answered curtly that there were no other gods.

He knew now for sure that he was being mocked. If they would not show him their god—if they had hidden him away in some shed, sack, or pit—he, Hivai, would have to go find him himself. And find him he would, and bring him a thanks-offering, and so be one of them at last.

Night after night, wrapped in his cloak, he stole out of his shack to prowl about the camp. Unseen, he foraged in old sacks, poked through piles of belongings, peered under plaits of onions, garlic, and beans, a man in search of god. He slipped past the snores of the sleepers and the sudden wingbeats of fowl that awoke briefly and then went back to sleep.

He kept it up for weeks. And yet, as if the desert had purged them of it all, he did not find a thing: not one image, statue, or idol. Not even an altar, or a stone hollowed for the blood. He flitted across the darkness, briefly silhouetted in the moonlit space between the houses before merging with the stone walls again. Not until a first pallor streaked the sky did he return to his hut, his heart beating hard.

One night he was caught. In the bright moonlight flooding the camp, a man had stepped outside to void himself. Squatting in the shadow of a wall, he saw Hivai's large figure start to slip away. When the man grabbed him, Hivai sought to break the man's grip. He was bigger than his pursuer, and the two were soon panting from exertion and fear. Catching hold of the hand that grasped him, he snapped the bones of several fingers and fled.

The shouts brought everyone running. They found him trembling, hiding behind the threadbare rugs in his hut. Their harsh voices sounded angry, betrayed. Marit stood triumphantly in her doorway, slowly running her hands over her hips. They would have thrashed him soundly on the spot had not Ahilud declared that justice was meted out by day, not by night. And so, tying him to a post, they went back to sleep.

In the morning three men brought him to the place of the trial. He stood there in sullen submission, not even trying to explain. He knew they would only laugh at him, mocking and incredulous. He knew, too, that they would cut off his right hand, as was the custom of the land. They were strong, he was weak, and justice was theirs. He did not even have a god in this place to defend him.

He awaited his judge. About a dozen men and women stood waiting too. He was sure the judge would be Ahilud, since it was his household he belonged to. Yet the man who came in the end was not Ahilud but Shirah. There was a hush when he appeared.

Shirah asked Hivai's accuser what it was that Hivai had stolen and tried hiding among his own possessions. Was it some bread? An article of clothing? Provisions of some sort? The man replied that naught had been stolen. The Gibeonite had taken nothing, for he had been timely discovered. Then, said Shirah, if no thing was taken, what punishment is due? You yourself say he stole not.

The onlookers nodded, exchanging whispers. Shirah's words were spoken truly. The Gibeonite had not stolen and therefore could not be punished. The verdict was just.

But Hivai's accuser was adamant. The Gibeonite has a wicked heart, he cried, holding up his hand to the crowd. Here, he broke these two fingers; he did it deliberately. The man is an evildoer.

Shirah asked the Hebrew if Hivai had lain in wait to kill him or break his fingers. No, said the man, it had happened while they were wrestling. But now his fingers were broken and he could not use them until the bones knit. Was it right that there be no indemnity?

There shall be indemnity, said Shirah. Let him pay you two kessita coins, a coin for each finger, for it happened while you wrestled. And now go home, both of you, for there is no blame in either.

All that day Hivai kept to his hut, like one who is ill. Now and then he stared at his right hand, as if to make sure that it was really there. He made a fist and opened it, made it again and slowly opened it once more, unable to believe his own fingers.

That evening Ahilud came to see him, sitting next to him on the rugs. Hemming and hawing with embarrassment, he told Hivai that there was no better worker than he in all Aner. But Marit did not approve of him; she insisted he go away. Though for years he, Ahilud, had stood firm as a rock against her, he was not young anymore; he was gray in the face from her complaints and no longer had the strength to resist. And besides, from now on every missing piece of string would be blamed on him by Marit, who would want to know how much longer she must put up with him. He, Ahilud, knew very well that Hivai had never laid a hand on anything. Not one straw, not one thread in his hut came from anyone else's kine, chattel, or land. There was not a more honest man in the village, and he, Ahilud, would deal honestly too, he would not take advantage of Hivai; no, he would pay him his full wage and even more; he would give him a suit of clothes and ten kessitas and a pair of good shoes, for he had served them faithfully for seven years. Let there be no bad blood between them.

Hivai nodded. Ahilud had spoken well. Hivai himself had thought to depart long ago, yet each time he had decided to sojourn a while longer, and lo, seven years had gone by. In the morning he would pack his things and go. Truly, Ahilud had taken no advantage and had done him no wrong. And he, Hivai, had served him faithfully, so that the covenant had been kept.

He fumbled in his belt and produced some scraps of cloth that were left from the day the covenant was sealed. Ahilud stared at them with emotion. He touched the faded bits of fabric. I have kept the words of the covenant, he said to Hivai. So you have, Hivai said to him. They looked at each other. The day the covenant was sealed their hair had been black, and now it was the hair of old men.

Ahilud's grandchildren walked him to the road. They waved to him. Good-bye, Hivai, they called, good-bye, Hivai.

He did not look back.

Hivai headed westward.

He walked slowly. He was not in any hurry. At first he bore the camp with him, still full of its sights and sounds. Something akin to sorrow, or at least to a sense of grievance, refused to go away. For seven years he had served them; he had taught them every trade and craft of the land; yet he had learned nothing from them in return. True, they had given him a just trial, and they had kept the words of the covenant. Yet there was something they had withheld from him, though he could not say what it was. He was leaving them the same man he had come. Seven years had passed as one day. Nothing had happened. A Gibeonite he had been, and a Gibeonite he still was.

Slowly, step by step, he began to regard his route more closely. The day seemed old and gray, although he could not say if what had aged was himself or the weary earth. The trees bore their fruit bleakly and the few flowers on the hillsides had a dull, gnawed look. The mountains and the sky lacked luster; the air was close, an unlifting cloud of grief.

A well-trodden path ran through the valley. Hivai was not alone on it. A man passed leading a donkey, on whose bolster sat a woman with a large fardel of twigs that stuck out on both sides. Some persons carrying a burden came toward him quickly, almost on the run. For seven years he had not descended from the mountain, and now here was this road and here were all these people.

The war had gone before him. Here and there by the roadside stood ruined houses and dead fruit trees with charred trunks and yellowed leaves. Once or twice he had to outwalk the smell of a corpse. He had no idea who had lived in these houses or who had destroyed them. He had no idea why the mountains looked so bleak.

Toward evening on the second day, as the sun was setting, he saw houses by the road. There were not enough of them to be a village. Several cows stood tethered to a trough, mooing at it softly, their hooves slithering on the wet ground. The fruit trees looked better here: there were figs and pomegranates, and a booth trellised with grapevines, from which hung heavy clusters of fruit. From inside what he realized was a breeding shed came a sound of bellowing. Several youths opened a wide door, through which they tried to pull a big black bull; its feet bound, its back muscles arched like a bridge, the animal lowered its head to the ground and refused to budge. A wreath of wilted laurel leaves hung from its neck.

Hivai stepped up and helped them pull the bull outside, holding it by its nose-ring. The boys thanked him, joking among themselves. He's already mounted eight cows, they explained in Canaanite, and he still wants more. He's a stud of studs, he was bought up north. You can't find bulls like him around here. Proudly, they kicked him a bit.

Hivai asked if there was anywhere nearby where he might find food and lodging. They pointed to a house among some trees. Let the traveler follow the smoke and the smells and they would bring him to the yard of an inn.

He entered, ducking his large head as he stepped through the doorway. The room was dark and smelled of wine and mutton. Hivai felt very hungry. Seating himself on a rug, he put down his pack. Three or four men were seated in the dim light at the other end of the room, gnawing on some bones before throwing them to a waiting dog that leaped up in the air to catch them, stretching its body string-taut and retracting it over its prize.

He sat resting for a while until a youth of about seventeen approached him with a basin of water. The boy's chest, which glistened with oil, was bare except for some black leather straps. More straps bound his arms. He walked like a dancer.

The boy knelt in front of Hivai and washed his feet, talking all the while. Surely the guest was weary from walking the mountains, he would feel better once his feet were washed and oiled. And should the guest want a woman, there was a harlot nearby, under the oak tree not far from the inn.

Hivai shook his head. He was too old, he said, his strength was no longer what it used to be. He hadn't had a woman in years. He shut his eyes as the hands massaged the soles of his feet, feeling his whole body relax. Perhaps tomorrow or the day after, he thought vaguely, he might visit the harlot after all to see if his strength was still with him.

While Hivai made himself comfortable, the youth took away the basin and returned with a pitcher of wine and some mutton and lentil stew. He stood by to serve him, balancing lightly on his feet and inquiring where the guest was from. He was a Gibeonite, said Hivai, though he had not been in that city for years and was now just passing through the land.

The youth's eyes lit up. Gibeon, he said reverently, was a city of brave warriors; he would like nothing better than to join them one day when he was a man. There was not another city like it among the kingdoms of the earth. The others had all been defeated, they had gone down like grass before that locust come from the desert; only Gibeon had resisted, unharmed despite its long siege. It had fought well and prevailed. He spoke with admiration, valiantly flexing his strapped biceps, his bare chest glistening with oil.

Hivai asked when all this had happened. That, said the youth proudly, was something he could tell him exactly: it had happened seven years ago. A great enemy had laid siege to Gibeon, but the city's gates had remained shut and it had held out. There had been traitors too, he could tell the guest about them also, there had been traitors in the city who were killed.

Who were the traitors? asked Hivai. He could not remember all their names, said the boy, dancing about on his feet, but one of them was even a judge. Shahar his name was, or Shaham, and another was called Yerubaal. Or perhaps it was Nerbaal. He would go ask his father, no one knew better than he. And there had been a prophet too, a great traitor, who had deserted to that abomination of a people, the Hebrews, and joined the enemies of his own city. It had been wise of the king to put him to death along with the treacherous elders. Might that be the fate of all enemies.

And what was the king's name? asked Hivai. He did not know the king's name, replied the youth, but when he had been in Gibeon at harvest time with all his father's house, he had seen him standing by the great pool; he was an albino, with a very red face. If the guest wished for more wine or bread he need only ask for it; it was a great honor to wait on one of the Gibeonites, whose bravery was famed throughout the land.

Hivai sat musing over his wine for a long while. The three men at the other end of the room kept drinking and talking in low voices; they laughed in low tones too, and then began to sing an unfamiliar ditty while slapping each other sottishly on the back. Hivai could not make out their faces in the darkness. They were sitting too far away and they never once looked in his direction.

The room grew darker. The youth returned with a large bundle of rolled-up rugs, spread them for the guests along the walls, and smoothed them out. Hivai lay down on his back, cradling his head in his hands. A solitary candle flickered in a wall niche, throwing a long shadow; then someone rose and blew it out.

Why, then, I am a dead man, thought Hivai in the darkness.

Morning found him ashen-faced outside the inn. He knew he could not stay in this place, yet he had nowhere to go. He was neither Gibeonite nor Hebrew. He was an outcast in the mountains, with nowhere to return to, no people, no city, no god. How great indeed must be his sin.

He walked on, dragging his feet. The road had already been taken by the war. Yet though the earth was still black from fire, here and there strong new shoots sprouted from dead tree trunks and outbursts of green patched the charred ground. The mountain was fighting back, the verdant life within it stubbornly bursting forth, trying to cover the ashes as if nothing had happened, as if there had been no devastation at all.

He had no idea how long he walked, carrying his pack on his back. Sometimes it seemed that it was all just one indeterminably long, exhausting dream before a morning that must come to find him in the end back in his old house in Gibeon, or on Ahilud's land. But the harsh dream went on and on. The road was well traveled; many people passed by on foot, sometimes leading beasts of burden; yet he scarcely bothered to look at them. What was there to see? Life for him was something that was over.

I am old, Hivai thought. An old man. And the gods of this country are all dead.

Toward evening he arrived at a crossroads. Some people were walking toward him, and he asked them where the main road led. It is the old road to Ai, they told him. The city is not far, though there is nothing there but ruins and some dwellers in the ruins. You won't find an inn there, or even a crust of good bread, because the ruin dwellers are dirt-poor.

He headed for Ai. It was almost dark when he arrived. The toothed wall of the city was still intact in parts, its jagged outline dark against the evening sky. No end of rubble lay on the slope beneath it: broken houses, broken roofs, broken stone, broken brick, broken clay, broken tile, broken glass clouded over and sightless. Here and there in this city of breakage burned little fires, over which families warmed their suppers.

He sat down on the rubble, which felt warm from the afternoon sun. Each time he moved or changed position the pile shifted under him, or brought new wreckage tumbling from above. There was no end of it. He took out the last wad of dried dates he had brought from Aner, tore off a handful of them, and began to eat.

After a while he was approached by a woman with a candle. Please, sir, she said, it would be a great honor if you joined my husband and sons and shared our meal with us. And bless you if you could give the little ones a few of those dates, because they haven't tasted a sweet in many a day.

She lit his way in the darkness here and there to keep him from stumbling. The family greeted him warmly. They were simple people.

He distributed the last of his dates to his hosts, who sucked on them slowly, careful not to swallow them too soon. They smiled at him.

Who had destroyed the mighty city of Ai? he asked the head of the family. Why ask, brother, answered the man, when we ourselves have forgotten. Six different times Ai was destroyed. A curse was upon it; there was no enemy or invader who did not level it anew, the Canaanite and the Amorite and anyone else you can name. It was each man against his brother on this mountain.

Hivai asked if the Hebrews had been there too. Yes, said the man. They were here and moved on. They fought treacherously, luring the defenders outside the gates and attacking them on open ground. But it was not they who destroyed the walls, he went on. The Hebrews are not a strong people, they come and go like locusts. It was the Amorites, they and their battering rams. But why sit speaking of the war? The war was there for all to see. No one was left in this entire city of ruins but themselves and a few other households, though perhaps the town might be rebuilt, since the countryside had survived. Behold, there was even a bit of green here and there, and perhaps the trees would once more give their fruit. Truly, where else could they go? There was no place for them anywhere on the mountain. They would stay where they were and hope for better times.

They went on talking for a while, the children staring at the newcomer until their eyes shut, after which all lay down to sleep on the rubble. Hivai rested his head on his bundle, watching the faraway stars wheel slowly through the sky.

That night Sahali came to him. Not the young woman he had sent off to Ai, but a small child, almost an infant. She looked at him with blazing eyes, hating him with all her might.

Why did she hate him so? he asked in wonderment. Had he not been good to her? Had he not bought her rings and anklets? Had he not sent her off to safety with an escort? Why, they both were dead now, she a dead child and he a dead prophet: how could the dead hate the dead?

But she went on sitting there and staring at him, hard and angular, her every word a curse. You spent your whole life making up to the gods, she mocked. The gods were all you ever cared about.

But against whom else can a man sin? he asked uncomprehendingly.

She rose and shouted at him that he did not understand a thing. Not one thing, she screamed, and was gone.

He felt a great weight bearing down on him.

When he rose in the morning everyone was asleep, each where he had lain down. They did not hear him leave. They were used to the crunch of footsteps on the rubble and were not awakened by them.

He was heading east now, with no way to get rid of the weeping building up inside him. His feet kept going by themselves, taking him ever eastward.

At last he reached a hill overlooking the Jordan. On his right was a high cliff, covered with scrub on its steep west side, where it faced the river. Down below, the river snaked back and forth, its banks dark with palm trees, a luxuriant thicket of green.

He descended to the rift of the Jordan. Between cliff and water lay a strip of bright sand, beyond which stood a thicket by the bank. There was not a human soul, just the trill of many songbirds in the treetops. The river blocked him one way, the cliff another. A ponderous heat oppressed the valley.

He cut some palm fronds, spread his cloak upon a branch, and made himself a shelter to rest in. He would go no further, he told himself, because he had nowhere further to go. He was an old man. A dead man. A fleeting shadow. No deed ever done by him upon the earth had done the least bit of good. Here let him live a while longer, here let him die, and here let his trials be over.

The place was good to him. A bit up the cliff, pheasants could be snared, and he laid out some animal traps too, though he rarely trapped anything big enough to eat. Sometimes he went down to the river, rolled up his sleeves, and fished with both hands. In time, peeling the fibers from the palm fronds, he learned to weave them into nets. Evenings were for resting, or for watching the mountains of Moab across the river turn purple and scarlet in the sunset. It was a godforsaken existence, and he liked it that way.

After a year or two he noticed that the traps had been empty for some time. At first he blamed the traps: they needed repair, the prey was getting away. But though he mended each of them, in the morning, when he went from trap to trap in the thick brush, the pits were empty and their concealment of twigs had been disturbed. It puzzled him greatly.

One day, as he was making his way through the thicket, he heard a sharp whistle close by. Looking up in alarm, he spied a small boy of seven or eight sitting half-naked in a hawthorn tree with a shepherd's pipe in his mouth. When he saw that he had been noticed, the boy leaned forward and whistled loudly again, right into Hivai's ear.

Hivai felt a wave of anger. The boy was teasing him, holding him up to ridicule like the clowning children in Gibeon. Their derision had followed him even here, to find him and destroy his peace of mind.

Blind with rage, he pulled the boy from the tree and cast him down by the throat with both hands. The boy stammered wordlessly, and when he opened his mouth to catch his breath, Hivai saw he had no tongue. It must have been cut out in one of the wars.

He released the boy, who jumped back on his feet at once and ran off with a heavy, muffled whimper, turning as he fled to pelt Hivai with branches, pebbles, dirt, whatever he could lay his hands on.

He knew now who had been stealing from his traps. Walking back to his shelter of palms, he sat down to think.

About a month later he saw the tongueless boy again. He was kneeling by one of the traps, inspecting its sharp stakes. His thin legs tensed to spring away as he heard Hivai approach, but Hivai called out that he would do him no harm.

The boy stood a ways off, his legs still poised for flight, his thin body breathing heavily. He was sunken-eyed and sickly looking. Hivai threw him a waterskin, which landed next to him. Afraid to bend down, he nudged it away with his foot, kicking it further and further until he judged the distance was safe. Even as he stood pouring water over his back, his eyes, dark with fright, never left Hivai for a moment.

Hivai told the boy to follow him to his shelter. Without waiting to see if he did, he turned around and walked ahead, tramping through the dry leaves on the sand. He could hear the boy's footsteps behind him, stopping and starting again.

But the boy was afraid to enter the shelter. A few feet from it he balked and ran away.

Not long afterward, Hivai heard steps in the leaves. The boy was in the doorway, looking too weak to either stand or sit. In the end he pitched forward, falling face down in the sand. His back was covered with infections and scratches where, driven crazy by the itching, he had scraped himself on the trunks of trees.

Hivai poured water over the feverish back. The boy shivered wordlessly.

That night the boy ran a fever and was delirious, emitting the heavy grunts of a mute. Hivai lay close by without moving. This one too will die, he thought, and wherefore then am I? He thought of finding a willow tree and decocting a salve from its leaves, but the idea seemed somehow shameful. Was he a Hebrew woman to sit blowing on a child's back? The boy would either live or die.

In the morning he was alive, though very pale. Hivai set out food between them. The boy would not eat, but he drank and drank with eager gulps. Then he put his pipe in his mouth, whistled a feeble thank you once or twice, and fell asleep. He slept all that day and all that night.

The next morning he was gone.

Once again Hivai was alone. The nights in the rift valley were getting cold; clouds from the west sailed overhead. Across the river the mountains of Moab were lost in the first light rain. One day he made up his mind and set out, climbing back into the mountains, into the land of men.

After two or three days he found a flock with its shepherd. They haggled at length. Hivai did not have many coins left in his belt and the shepherd was stubborn. He drove a hard bargain, even rounding up his flock and walking off while Hivai followed pleadingly after him.

In the end they split the difference. Hivai bought a pregnant ewe and a pair of goats. He tied them together with a rope and headed back for his shelter.

The boy was sitting in the doorway when he arrived. He jumped to his feet when he saw Hivai, piping short, high whistles of joy; then, spying the goats and the sheep, he blew with all his breath one more, very long whistle of excitement. Sternly, Hivai made him stop. Instead of deafening a person, why didn't he make himself useful and untie the tired animals and water them? He even gave the boy a name: Gosha. At first he didn't know why. Then suddenly, as if an intricate knot had slipped open inside him, he remembered: why, that was the name of his brother, his little brother who had been sacrificed before his eyes in the temple in Gibeon, cast into the flames when he wasn't yet five years old. He must have always known that name, must have remembered it all along.

The boy Gosha didn't seem to mind. Perhaps it really was his name, or perhaps he just happened to like it. He lingered a while in the shelter, feeding the ewe and the goats while making little noises to himself, and ran off. Hivai noticed that in his absence the boy had stolen a rug. He swore a bit but hadn't the strength to be angry. The trip had exhausted him.

Each morning he descended to the river to fill the waterskins, walking slowly because his old legs were not so spry anymore. The evening chills made every joint ache. He had to force himself to wade into the water in order to pull in the nets. At night he made a fire and huddled close to it, his legs hurting him no matter how still he lay.

Prophecy returned to him too, the small, harmless prognostications of old men. He knew when it would rain on the mountains across the river, funneling down from the gray storm clouds. He knew which date palm would bear the first fruit, and what he would find when he opened his traps, a lizard, mouse, or jackal cub. They pleased him, these prophecies, like small, humble blessings. Once he dreamed of the great pool in Gibeon, but felt no fear. He knew he would never return.

When Gosha came to visit he chided him cantankerously, like an old man. In reply the boy merely grunted. He must make sure to come down with him to the river each morning, said Hivai, because he was too old to carry the waterskins and empty the nets by himself. How long would Gosha eat the bread of idleness and go on stealing from the traps? He knew the boy's evil ways and manners; if Gosha would not help him each morning, let him not set foot in the shelter.

Gosha listened stolidly, then turned and went. It was not for him.

Yet one morning he was there, leaning on a stick and piping short whistles to call Hivai. Without a word the two went down to the river.

After that, he came every morning. The ewe gave birth in the spring. The boy was fond of her milk, sometimes stealing it from the lambs and guzzling it before their eyes. Their trips to the river took a long time, for Hivai's legs could barely carry him. He leaned on the boy both going and coming, careful not to hurt his old scars. Once he cut some good reeds by the river, brought them back to the shelter, and threw them in a corner among some pots and rags.

The sunsets turned the mountains of Moab to gold in a broad

flood of light that spanned both horizons over mountain and water and copses of tall palms. They sat watching while the light retreated slowly up the mountain, gathering the train of its radiant dress, and the earth of the valley released the day's heat with a smell of bulrushes and fish and much water.

Perhaps next winter, he told the boy Gosha, perhaps even this year, he would take the good reeds and make them both flutes.

AFTER
CHILDHOOD

In a small stone hut, not far from the Valley of Zin, lived a young man whose father had sought to kill him. Ever since then his eyes blinked rapidly, as if fending off a strong light.

The villagers kept away from him and he from them, their speech brief and halting, no more room in it for good or evil than the space between a cloud and a lone thorn tree in the desert.

Not many people lived in the village. A generation or two back, several families from the mountains had wandered there in search of peace, going south and south again, skirting the armed convoys of soldiers that sometimes galloped to a nearby district capital, and the bands of hungry marauders, war-weary like themselves. For ten years the people of the mountains had fought each other, each man for himself, each coveting the other's pasture. Many had left. Those who owned land clung to it stubbornly, their anger brooding over it. Those who did not took angrily to the roads and roamed with their women and children, plundering and lamenting. One had to go a long way to escape them. Their faces dusty and bronzed, they popped suddenly from behind rocks and carob trees, up to no good.

There was evil on the mountain roads. Few traveled them.

They kept heading south with their flocks. Days and months passed and their legs plodded on by themselves. The mountains shrank to hills, the hills to desert flatland. And still they pressed on, as if fearing to stop as long as they still met a single wayfarer. The grass had grown sparser too.

In the end they reached a dry gully. Many dark stones lay in its bed, tumbled by a cascade of water that had thundered down from the hills long ago, frightening away all life. Now they lay aridly, slowly buried in sand like old tombstones warped by time. Over them hung the shadows of the hills and a great silence.

The travelers dropped to the ground, too weary to take another step. A few pushed on to the top of a large cliff and came back dully. As far as the horizon, they reported, were dry white hills, a wasteland, no life in it.

They knew they would go no further. Nor did they have the strength to. Dragging the dark stones one by one up the slope, they built huts for themselves and their children and fences for the flocks. At night they sank into sleep as into a thick woods; they woke not knowing where they were, frightened by so much emptiness. There was no one else for miles around.

Little by little, they got used to it. The sheep found some pasture and stood cropping it beneath the burning sun. Women found mallow plants to cook. The desert wind smoothed the worry lines from their faces.

There was plenty of water a day's walk away, but there was no getting at it. A large garrison was stationed there, mercenaries serving in Pharaoh's army, with a lookout day and night in the tower of a small fort. They collected the caravan tax from the camel trains that crossed two or three times a year from beyond the Jordan Valley to Gaza or Sharuhen. It took courage to look in their direction.

Here in the hills they made do with what little rain there was. They quickly learned to build small dams and channels to capture each drop. Fruit trees, they found, grew in the bed of the gully that was empty most of the year; a bit of wheat was sown on terraces laboriously walled against the flash floods that carried off the young stalks in the springtime, sometimes even a lamb or child. Poor and envious, they quarreled over their small strips of land that were no more than a few paces wide.

But the rain refused to be harnessed. Sometimes it came in sudden, muddy bursts that smashed the dams like a giant crushing straw, swept everything away, and disappeared. Sometimes it tarried for years. In the bottomland the tamarisks and broom kept on growing, along with a few palms and an occasional stooped, skinny almond. Higher up there was nothing.

Often they stared greedily at a dark rain cloud passing overhead, watching with longing as it dropped its load far away on the garrison by the water hole. Sometimes, seized by despair, a man ran to his flock, snatched a young goat, covered it with his cloak as though ashamed of his staring children, and bounded quickly up to the flat top of a hill to offer a sacrifice in time. Perhaps the people had sinned, perhaps they had forgotten the Law given to Moses on Sinai. They had no prophets, they had no kings, God was no longer with them as in the great days in the great desert, let there be a sin-offering, let the cloud bestow its bounty. Now.

Sometimes it rained a little. Sometimes they went thirsty. They knew that God was far away. Perhaps he was in the mountains, the place of the priests and the tabernacle.

Salu was about twelve when his father took a knife to him. He dimly remembered lying there, bound with strong sparrowwort cords, dead for a long time. Then he rose to find himself alone in the world, a huge sun overhead, and a slaughtered, stiff-legged lamb, smeared with blood and flies, at his side. Blinking, he staggered off into the desert, falling and rising and falling again all that day, and perhaps all that night, perhaps the day doubled and became two days. He walked on and on, not knowing where or why.

Someone found him and took him home. He drank some water from the jug and fell asleep. He was alone in the house.

The villagers felt ashamed. They did not like to talk about it. A mad dog, a dreamer, they said about Salu's father, today every flea says, I'm Abraham, God tells me what to do in my dreams. Such things aren't done among us. They spat as if to get rid of an unclean taste. It's not our way. Only a madman would sacrifice his own son like the boors of the land.

When Salu approached them, they fell silent. He did not do so often.

He barely remembered his mother. Once he summoned the courage to ask an old woman about her. She regarded him uneasily, then began a long story about uncles, his mother's brothers, who had come one day from afar to take his mother home because she had not been properly given away, the bride price had not been paid. When it was paid, she would return. Meanwhile, Salu should not grieve; were not the village women as good to him as ten mothers? Let Salu take a date, see how sweet it was.

He did not know why he didn't believe her. Once, in the pasture, a boy told him that his mother's body had been found beneath the cliff. She had tripped and killed herself chasing a sheep, the boy said. The whole village knew.

Salu did not believe that, either. For a long while he struggled to remember whether his mother had disappeared before the sacrifice or after, but in the end he gave up. It was all part of a fear too big and strong to bear. He liked to think that his mother had been taken to the fort by the water; a passing Egyptian horseman had seized her and held her prisoner there. She wanted to return to her son and could not. Whenever his sadness was too much for him, he sat staring at the fort on the horizon, imagining he heard her voice. Once or twice, when a strong breeze blew from there, he felt her hand stroke his head and cried for a long time.

He lived in the house with his father. Where else was he to go. All day long he tended their small flock, from morning till the ebbing of the light, whose great sheet was rolled into a thin red line on the horizon that paled and vanished. With nightfall the first cold struck the desert, piercing his clothes. The sheep huddled and turned their tails to the wind, bleating for home.

Mostly he slept in the hut. Sometimes, when the desert winds were especially cold, he curled up amid the warm, woolly bodies of the flock. Blinking and meek, he tended with the passing of the years to the sick old man, bringing him milk, rubbing his aching feet, baking bread for him on hot coals. He was his father.

When Salu came home from pasture one day to find that his father was dead, he did not think of going to the village for help. Dragging the corpse to a sandy mound, he steadily dug the grave. The corpse was heavy and stiff, evil to touch.

Four or five villagers saw him digging. By the time they arrived, the body was covered with sand. Salu went on piling on more and more of it, not knowing when to stop. He had never buried anyone before. Big stones were put on the grave to keep off the wild animals. No one could bring himself to say a consoling word. Salu said nothing either. In the end they all went home.

Alone in the house, it took him a while to stop fearing the stiff, gray body. It had already been cold and hard when his father was ill. Once he dreamed that his father had returned to life. He was back in his bed and Salu knew that he would have to grit his teeth and rebury him. This time he would pile heavier stones on the grave. He awoke in a rage.

He was now old enough to be talked about by the villagers. Perhaps they felt guilty for having left him alone so many years. We have to find Salu a wife, they said. He's a grown boy and shouldn't be by himself. Soon he will fornicate with the sheep and goats and the abomination will be upon us all.

Yet they knew that no one would offer Salu his own daughter. Their old, obscure fear of the boy and his family continued to haunt them. A queer lot, the family was, and more than they could cope with. Salu was not like other youngsters. He blinked. Perhaps God had struck him with the staggers or the squint. And there was his mother. And his crazy father. Perhaps the whole seedline was cursed. No one could know. Better for him to marry out.

It did no good to point out that his flock was the best in the village, that his plot was fenced like a fortress. The secret had seeped into them all, as old as the world itself.

In the end they agreed. When Hiram went again to the mountains to trade with the upland towns, he would bring Salu a wife from one of the families that had remained there. Perhaps Salu had kin from whom the bride could be taken. Hiram must not tell them the secret, though; he was a wise man and would keep it to himself, lest the mountain folk deny Salu their daughters. Say nothing, Hiram, the villagers said with honeyed lips, you can tell them his name but no more. Wives come from God and God will decide.

But Hiram tarried. A year came and went and the village remained shut on itself. Although people needed new blades for their plows, and wine, honey, oil, and dried figs, and brides-to-be were waiting for their jewelry, he was not in any hurry. In another month, perhaps two, he said to those who pressed him. Now is not a time for travel. The sun is too hot. The oil in the mountains is old, from last year's harvest. Honey costs more than gold. When the days grew short he would set out.

They knew he mustn't be pestered. He would go or not go as he pleased. Sometimes he went nowhere for years.

One day a small boy came to Salu's house, his cheeks flushed from running. He had trouble getting out the words. Quick, Salu, quick, he said, the old men are calling you, they're under that palm tree down there, quick, Salu, come, Salu.

He started down into the gully, wondering.

Some ten men were sitting on a low, flat mound of sand, from which grew a gnarl of tamarisk trees, thornbushes, and a sparse, twisted palm. They looked pleased with themselves.

Salu greeted them and waited. He blinked quickly, hanging his head.

Hiram, they told him with ribald laughter, was about to set out and would fetch him a wife. First, however, he had to give Hiram a bride price, gifts or money, so that he could bring home a comely bride. And Salu must prepare his house for her, with fresh bedding and a place for her dresses. The mountain women have lots of dresses and shirts of many colors, they said laughing.

He stared at them, fearing mockery. But their eyes were not unkind. They waited for him to thank them, to jump up and down and clap his hands or bend to kiss the folds of their cloaks.

He stood there. The elders bantered a little more. They trusted him, they said, to act like a man. They knew he was a straight shot with a bow and would not disgrace them with the mountain woman or let her put on airs. They were haughty, the mountain women. He must remember to tread hard on this one's foot before taking her as his wife.

As soon as he saw they had run out of words, Salu took his leave. They watched him go disappointedly, as if he had spoiled the jest.

Salu had no notion where to get the bride price. He spent the day confusedly, forgetting each moment what he had planned the moment before. That night, he remembered: in the storage space, covered by old straw mats, cracked jars, and bundles, were some sacks of his parents' belongings. They hadn't been looked at in years. Perhaps he would find a bride price there.

He lay awake all night, waiting for morning. Once or twice he thought that the high peaks in the east were pinkening, but it was only the moonlight, high, bright, and deceiving. He thought he heard voices in the house; there was no one there. A gerbil scratched at the threshold and was gone.

And then the birds called the light forth with strong, menacing cries, darting through the sky with sharp impatience as if running thin ropes to haul up the sun. Sounds of awakening came from the village. A smell of smoke mingled with the scent of fresh bread.

Salu went to the storage space. It took a long while to move all the sacks. He could not say why he had left them unopened for so many years. Most contained nothing but moth-eaten rags and broken, useless pottery. Their old, musty smell made him cough.

It angered him unaccountably, the sight of all his father's and mother's cast-off things. Clouds of moths and dust, the leftovers of death, blew through the rents in the fetid cloth. The cloth crumbled in his hands like a fistful of smells.

In one of the sacks he found something hard wrapped in old fabric. Quickly he unrolled it. There were two small anklets, big enough for a child's foot, and a tarnished copper mirror. And beneath, a scent locket. A last perfumed trace adhered to it, the essence of another life.

He squatted for a long while, wonderingly inhaling the trace of scent, holding the anklets in his palm, until he understood: his mother had been but a girl when brought to this place, a child bride. He tried slipping an anklet onto his arm but could not get it past his first three fingers.

The fingers remained faintly scented. He shut his eyes and tried to remember. Dimly he thought he saw a young girl, not yet fully grown, running out of the house with scratched cheeks as if she had clawed herself. She was sobbing and held her arms out in front of her. There was no one in the whole desert to help her.

He could remember no more. The vision oppressed him. He wasn't sure of it. He wasn't sure of any of the dreams that sometimes came to him.

He ran his hands over his face to compose himself. Then, blinking strongly, he rose, dragged the rotting sacks from the storage space, piled them on top of each other, and brushed off his hands. After a moment's thought, he fetched some hot coals from the firepit in the yard with a small shovel and set the dry pile ablaze. It burned quickly. When nothing was left he cleaned out the storage space, fumigating it with smoke. Empty and purified, it made him feel better, as if he were rid of a heavy burden he had not known he was carrying.

He wrapped the anklets and mirror carefully. He did not look at himself in the mirror.

At midday he went to see Hiram.

Men crowded around Hiram's house, from which came a great din. As if invited to a celebration, loud-voiced children came and went and ran about gaily. The whole village had turned out to watch Hiram prepare his camels for the trip and rig their packs. He was a master; no one could load a camel like Hiram. Every few minutes one of his sons stepped outside with a new bundle. People came and went, leaving merchandise and messages. Hiram's sons sat in the covered doorway, counting each pouch and haversack.

The two big camels stood nodding their heavy heads and pawed the ground, from time to time letting out huge, flatulent grunts, putting first one thin leg and then the other forward, as if unsure whether their large hulks would follow once they started out. Children decorated their saddles and bridles with bits of cloth, scampering off whenever one of them turned his head around with a grunt and bared huge teeth from which dripped a yellow slobber. The boldest jabbed the camels' feet with sharp sticks and ran off. The camels, big and stolid, went on standing there.

Salu stepped up to Hiram, the package in his hand. Blinking meekly, he asked if it would do for a bride price.

Hiram regarded him quietly and weighed the items first in one hand and then in the other. He would take the anklets, he said at last, because they were gold. They had no ornaments, no buds or flowers or the like, but they were gold and would do. The mirror could stay with Salu. It wasn't burnished, perhaps because the copper was poor, and had no value.

Salu listened, spellbound. Hiram had spoken truly, without jesting or hemming and hawing, as a man speaks to a friend. Calling on two witnesses, he wrapped the anklets in the cloth and proclaimed in a loud voice that they were the property of Salu and were for the purchase of a wife. Should God not cause his trip to prosper, or should brigands plunder him and his sons, he was quit of blame before Salu.

The witnesses said "Amen" loudly and Hiram resumed squatting on his haunches and turned to the next customer. The transaction was an involved one, having to do with some doves and jars of honey, and Salu paid no attention.

Only now did he realize that he could not turn back. A wave of fear passed over him.

The villagers smiled at him. Some clapped his shoulder: So, Salu, you'll be a husband, you'll father many boys for us. A few of the young girls glanced his way as if seeing him for the first time. True, he blinked, but no one looked more manly from behind. A brief sorrow flitted through their gazes.

Impatient, he made his way past them. What's done is done, he kept telling himself unbelievingly. What's done is done. He didn't know if he was happy or sad. His heart pounded strongly, as if he had run a long way.

He returned home to his chores, many things on his mind.

The whole village rose the next morning to see Hiram off. All admiringly watched him tie the last bundles, adding more and more sacks, bags, and jars, which he kept rearranging, until at last everything was tied with strong twine. The large, patient camels knelt on the ground, their bridles decorated, their heavy heads wagging to the left and to the right, their dripping jaws working away. Their baggage bulged on either side of them.

It was time to move out. Hiram's sons swung into the saddles after their father and brought the camels to their feet with loud cries. First to rise were the animals' long necks, high above the rest of them; then came the rear legs, so thin it was hard to believe they could support such a load. The crowd let out a sigh. The camels pawed the ground leg after leg, eager to be under way.

The small caravan set out and passed the last huts, swaying heavily. All knew it would not soon be back. Mothers lifted small children in the air to see Hiram head out onto the plain, where the breeze that was waiting as usual covered the tracks of the caravan with sand. The world stretched into the distance as far as the eye could see.

Salu stood watching too. A sort of apathy settled over him. The caravan was gone, but what was it to him. Who knew if Hiram would return before winter. Who knew if he would return at all. When the swaying camels reached the tops of the hills, from which they looked small, distant, and unknown, he turned and headed home.

U p in the hills, the air was different. The camels followed a twisting trail, plodding slowly, giving the Jebusite villages a wide berth. Once they were stopped by a patrol. Hiram leaped down from his camel, prepared for the worst. He talked and talked, now and then laying his hand on his heart, while the soldiers listened in silence. Then, with a grovel or bow, he laid a few coins before them and remounted. The soldiers let them move on.

Hiram's sons looked around them with cublike, inquisitive eyes, sniffing the new air that smelled of thyme and scabwort. They saw each day tread the haze of the plain and drive it deeper into the ground, which turned from yellow to gray and from sandy to solid. Hills rose on either side of the trail, higher and higher, carob, olive trees, and thickets of terebinths growing from the rocks. They breathed the smells warily, filling their lungs and listening to their own breaths. The air taught them the ways of the mountain.

And then at last, on a hilltop to their right, they saw a cluster of houses, each tucked tight above the other, supporting its shoulder or flank; take away one of them, so it seemed, and the entire village would topple. The sun was low in the west. A flood of golden light bathed the mountains.

The place looked nothing at all like their hardscrabble huts with their walls of loose, black stone, scattered in the desert like the thorn trees, one here and two over there. The mountain stone was different, too. It was the color of human flesh.

Hiram pointed. Ma'aleh Hoglah, he said. The caravan halted, the camels grunting and snorting, their heads wagging in front of their motionless bodies as if not wanting to stop. They had to be gripped tightly by their nose rings.

A large garden planted with walnut trees surrounded a well. There were pomegranates too. The younger of Hiram's sons climbed wonderingly down to touch their stiff, waxy flowers. Pomegranates he had seen, but never their blossoms. They made him think of little red jugs.

A warm welcome awaited them at Issachar's. Issachar came forth in person from the village to greet them and gave Hiram a hearty embrace. Then he led them back to his house, issuing orders while skipping nimbly up the rocky slope, clutching at fig branches for support. Slaughter lambs. Fetch water. Get a move on.

They passed the evening in Issachar's courtyard, which was shared with his brothers who lived in the surrounding houses. Visitors kept arriving, each kissing Hiram's cheeks and beard. Women came to ask about their kin. Were they still alive? Did they have children and grandchildren? There was a babble of voices.

Hiram's sons huddled close to each other, stuffing themselves in silence. The food tasted strange. The words were different too, quicker and sharper, as if tossed up and down the mountain slopes; people waved their arms when they spoke. They did not dare look at the giggling girls who kept bringing bowls and stacks of bread. Feeling laughed at, they hurried to their pallets when it was time for bed and covered their heads with their cloaks. They did not even bother to check where the camels had been put for the night. They were afraid. The darkness was darker in the mountains, as in a dungeon.

Hiram sat on the seller's mat for four days, from morning till night, delivering what he had been asked to and selling dates, copper, cloth, and precious Egyptian stones. He had a few good household gods with him too, if anyone wanted them. Once, in former years, there had been whispered requests for them, but no one seemed to want them anymore, except one woman, who bought a pair of them, hid them in her things, and hurried off.

The mountain people were more eager to talk than to buy. Were there Canaanites in the south? they asked. Were there judges, or kings, or prophets? Here there were prophesiers everywhere, men of little worth who went around ranting like the lowest of the low, they tore the hair from their beards, but no one knew what they said because they mumbled. No, the mountain men answered Hiram, they had no judge. Each man did as he saw fit. He could see that they lived well. Their only complaint was the Canaanites. And from the Canaanites God would surely save them. God was good.

Hiram's sons stared at the ground, dripping scorn. How could anyone here even know if the Canaanites were coming? There was no plain on which marauders could be seen from afar. There was only peak after peak, wooded and concealing. The Canaanites would catch all of them unawares and carry them off like eggs from a nest.

On the fifth day of his visit Hiram spoke with Issachar and his brothers about Salu.

They turned him down politely. Not that they had anything against the desert dwellers. Why, they were brothers, flesh of one flesh, they spoke the same language and thought the same thoughts—to whom but their kinfolk should they give their daughters if they did not want them to cast eyes on the young men of the countryside? But the roads, they apologized, were too dangerous: there were mounted patrols, and bandits, and Canaanites lurking around each bend. And their daughters were pampered, too; they were not used to hard work, of which there was much in the desert, fences to be built and cisterns to be dug until one was black in the face, yes, yes, they knew, they had heard: a year's rains there could be cupped in the palm of one hand.

They sniffed delicately as if scenting the odor of sweat, too well-behaved to put their fingers to their nostrils. Certainly, Hiram and his sons could stay with them as long as they liked. They would want for nothing; they were guests, the blessed of God, like the angels who visited Abraham. Perhaps next year Hiram would bring the young man, this Salu, to Ma'aleh Hoglah. He would be sure to find a wife here and live well.

Indeed, said one of the mountain men with a laugh, perhaps Hiram's sons would stay too. They came from a good family and would easily find wives. And they were so handsomely tanned from the sun, too, more burnished than the copper they had brought.

Although there was no malice in their words, Hiram's face fell. They have become fat and soft, these men, he thought. No good will come of them. The hint of an affront hung in the air.

He decided to return sooner than he had planned.

The next evening, when the mountain was its most golden, he was approached by a maiden. She was about sixteen, tall, with big feet. She must have been stalking him, biding her time until he was alone.

He had noticed her the day they had arrived. She had a way of keeping to herself, hugging the corners of the house and staying aloof from Issachar's other girls. He saw, too, that she was secretly following him and his sons, watching them from the corners all the time. Once he saw her go furtively to the camels and grip one fearlessly by the nose ring, studying its braided bridle with what seemed an expert eye. She fled when she saw him.

Now she stood before him, done hiding. Looking him straight in the eye, she said that she would go with him.

He was much taken aback. Was she unhappy here? he asked. She shook her head firmly several times: no, no, she was not. She was the daughter of Issachar's younger brother, who had turned her mother out for being unloved, which was why she had no brothers or sisters. But she could work as well as any boy and she would go with Hiram. She did not cajole or make eyes like the other girls. Her speech was direct.

He said he would speak to Issachar. She nodded and left, tall and as sure of herself as if she had tied him to her with a rope.

As he reached Issachar's house it occurred to Hiram that he had not asked the girl what her name was. How would they know whom he meant? But at once they guessed. That's Moran, they said, Moran, Issachar's niece. They had forgotten all about her because her mother was unloved, and she would not inherit from her father.

Quickly they recovered from their surprise. If Hiram thought she was a match for the young man he had spoken of, it must be from God; they would do as he requested, for he was their kin. Yes, so they would, though he was taking the best of their daughters, the most beloved of them all, there wasn't a better maiden in the mountainland. Far be it from them to oppose God's decision. It only remained for her father to ask her if she agreed, for that was the custom: no maid was forced to marry against her will.

She did not have to be searched for very hard. She was sitting outside, a few steps away, her back to the wall of the house, tracing in the dust a bridal veil strung with coins. She jumped up and erased it when she saw her father approach.

She would go with Hiram, she said.

The news put an end to the awkwardness. Men went over to slap Hiram's back—you see, we are marrying with you, Hiram, there will always be a covenant between us. Issachar ordered more banquets. Boys brought doves and slaughtered them in the yard. Hiram went to his camels and opened more bundles. Soon everything was sold. The smell of blood mingled with the clink of weighed silver.

Moran was not given a camel to ride, nor a bondwoman or a servant to accompany her. The mountain people were busy. Issachar's brother had gone to the villages to buy oil and no one knew when he would return. Issachar apologized profusely when Hiram asked how Moran would travel without a camel. He had been too occupied to think of it, but now he would give Moran a she-ass, the finest that he owned, and money to buy a camel on the way. She would reach her husband looking like a queen.

The she-ass was produced. The money was forgotten. Moran's sisters hurriedly sewed her a veil and festooned it with coins. Embarrassed, she tried it on. She did not know what to do with all the gifts she had been given: embroidery, flaxenwear, mandrake root for desire, scabwort for conception, olive oil for soft skin. She stood facing the merrily giggling girls, who kept wanting to caress her, her feet looking larger and flatter than ever.

T hen Hiram's caravan headed down from the mountains.

Moran rode at the head. Bright-eyed, she sat between the saddlebags, thirstily watching the landscape unfold into a new, endless world that began where the mountains dropped off, no more than placid hills now, covered with sparse grass, warmed by a breeze from the south.

She could not stop looking around her. Perhaps all her life she had thirsted for a place like this. She felt herself opening up to it. The flatlands took her in easily, as if she had always belonged to them. Each morning she rose excited, every breath and warm breeze buoying her body with life. The sky above was vast enough to float in. Never had she felt so good before. The world was simple and right: the wind, the way her foot met the ground, the silence around her. It was as if there were nothing she could not do, nothing that was beyond her.

When they camped she stood with her head high, nostrils flaring, not knowing what to do with all the strength filling her. At night she did not sit with the men, their red faces glowing from the campfire. Striding off among the high, fierce stars, she took in the tenuous sadness of the desert with its thin light spread over the dunes. When the moon was out, it was almost too much to bear. For the first time in her life she heard total silence, the quiet of before-and-after-all-things. The soft, low hills crouched unawakened, walked on by neither man nor beast, though perhaps these once had been here and were forgotten. Life was strong in this place.

Hiram did not take the Sharuhen trail. Since he and his camels were laden with money and goods, he chose to bypass Beersheba from the east. Once they spied a quickly moving caravan in the distance and took cover behind a contour of earth, tugging the camels to their knees. Hiram's sons gripped their daggers, but the marauders did not spot them. Or else they were unworthy of a chase.

Another time, at midday, when Moran went off to relieve herself, Hiram's younger son appeared behind her half-timid and half-lustful, his face burning. Quickly she scooped some sand and crammed it into her sex with a mocking stare. He thought better of it and slunk away, scared to death she might tell his father. She did not. Her scratched vagina hurt for a few days and was healed.

The boy did not look at her again for the rest of the journey.

South of Beersheba, the air grew strange. A stiff wind blew all night, whipping the sand into a thick haze. Behind it an oozing sun, as if bursting from the heat, had lost its shape. The faded world was as gray as an autumn day.

Hiram studied the horizon worriedly and made them dismount in a thicket of zyzyph trees. There was a whirlstorm coming. Soon it would hit them and their animals.

The sky grew black. It was dark and very hot. The air was full of sand.

They stood wrapped in their cloaks beneath a large tree, covering as much of their heads and bodies as they could. The animals brayed restlessly. The wind gusted wildly and the nearby dunes ran like water, vanishing and reappearing again before their eyes. The sand beneath their feet shifted too. They gasped for breath beneath their cloaks. Nothing could be heard above the scream of the wind.

Moran could not get enough of it. She would have run clear-eyed into the wind had not Hiram called her angrily back. A sand spout shot skyward, revolving madly like a column on its base and spinning off into the desert. More spouts whirled around them. Then one struck. They shut their eyes, the wild, smothering geyser of sand sucking them up by their billowing cloaks. The animals lowed with fear.

Then, as fast as it came, it was gone. The blow had been a glancing one. The wind spun away. Slow drops of rain began to fall, starting and stopping like the patter of many birds' feet on a roof. At first the choking feeling grew worse and the veins bulged in their foreheads; then, slowly, the rain beat down the sand, clearing vents for air. The desert was bleak and wintry, hung with heavy sheets of wet grit that blocked the horizon. The sand was stilled and rivulets of water now ran over it, gurgling restlessly from the high ground.

The storm was over. They shook the sand from their cloaks. The large zyzyph tree that had sheltered them was buried halfway up its trunk by a mound that hadn't been there before. Throats and bodies parched, they downed great droughts of water, frantically quenching their own thirst and the animals' as if there were nothing to do in the world but gulp, swallow, and burp until waterlogged.

Moran shook the sand from her long hair and kept wiping her eyes, about to burst from so much life. A great wave of joyous laughter came over her and spread to the others. Filthy and smeared with wet sand, they howled wildly. Hiram joined too, his belly shaking. That was the devil's own fart, he guffawed. The devil's own fart.

They stood staring at their new surroundings. Rearranged by

the wind, the dunes looked unfamiliar. For a moment they thought they were lost. But Hiram knew the way.

They were drawing close to the High Negev. Sensing they were near home, the camels stepped up the pace with fresh strength. The travelers relaxed. Many crows dotted the landscape, hopping on the sand with brusque expectation. Hiram's sons threw them crumbs and the chewed husks of dates. The crows are holy, they told Moran. We are blessed by them. It was they who drove out the old gods that lived here, the Baal and the Ashera. If not for the crows, we would still be worshipping them, and we and our children would be sinners. They emptied their foodbags of dry crusts, parched barley, and dried chick-peas. The crows swooped down with shrill cries, lords of the domain.

Hiram was not pleased. This is no way to bring a bride to her husband, he thought, riding barefoot on a she-ass ahead of the camels like a tomboy. He signaled the caravan to stop and re-form, but Moran would not hear of it. Digging her heels into the donkey's flanks, she spurred it into a gallop. Although he could have caught up with her and insisted, he yielded. A smile crossed his face as he thought of her running toward the whirlstorm.

It occurred to him that he had never presented her or her father with the anklets, and they halted again. He rummaged through the saddlebags, taking out and putting back items until he found, groping deep, the cloth package given him by Salu. He handed it to Moran.

She regarded the little gold hoops without knowing what to do with them. Her feet were bigger than Salu's mother's. In the end she jammed the anklets onto her wrists so tightly that she could not get them off again and spent the rest of the day looking at them. Her hands, no longer simple, seemed not to belong to her. She was not sure she wanted the gift.

They were nearing the village when, speaking quickly without meeting her eyes, Hiram told her the story of the boy whose father had tried to kill him and whose mother had either fallen or thrown herself from a cliff. Salu was not like other men. He was a blinkard.

Her face grew tender as she listened.

They could have reached the village that evening, but Hiram held them back. He did not want to arrive like a thief in the night. On the opposite hillside were some crooked stone structures hovered over by crows that Moran thought was the village, until told it was an old Canaanite graveyard. She shuddered, pityingly eyeing the cracked stones. Those beneath them, she thought, feared more in death than in life. She spent the night bereft of sleep.

In the morning, as soon as the sun rose above a clump of tamarisk trees, they quickly covered the last stretch.

In broad daylight Moran entered Salu's house. He was not home.

Five or six women had assembled to welcome her with broad smiles. Salu had gone to the fort, they told her. He would be back the next day. She should lie down to rest and let them wash her dusty feet, for the house was hers. They never stopped beaming, as if to make up for her absent husband.

She glanced around her, pleased by the bareness. Salu had cleaned up well. From the center of the ceiling, crawling with bugs, hung a fly trap of sparrowwort dipped in honey. She untied the slithering glob and threw it as far outside as she could.

The chattering women kept coming and going, bringing bowls of cooked food, almonds, and dates, looking excitedly at her possessions, pawing through the open bundles as if they owned them. It was evening before they left. Moran did not know what to answer when they asked about God in the mountains. There is a tabernacle not far from Ma'aleh Hoglah, she replied. And priests. On feast days we send them gifts. But it's not anything we talk about.

That surprised them. They had thought there was more God in the mountains.

When they were gone, she went over to one of her bags and saw that her best embroidery was gone. Stolen.

No matter, she told herself. She lay down on the clean pallet, aching from the trip.

Slowly, the house cooled off. The thorn trees had as though edged closer. For a moment she imagined she was back in the mountains with her sisters chatting nearby and a servant at work at the spinning wheel, the cry of a baby coming from next door. But there were no such sounds. The wind blew through the chinks in the stone walls as if nothing were there, and the cold desert night crept in with it. There was nowhere to hide from it.

She rose and plugged the walls with empty sacks. The anklets got in her way.

She waited for Salu. In the morning a boy came to take the flock to pasture and she went with him to do the milking and make clabber. She set some flour out in the sun, prepared water, painted her eyes with antimony, and went on waiting.

In the end she asked a woman where Salu was. Reluctant to answer, the woman looked away. Then she leaned toward Moran and said: He's gone to the Hittites, there's a camp of them near the fort, a couple of families, worthless, shiftless folk, the men can be had for the sole of a shoe and the women for a handful of figs. Salu goes there to eat and drink, he has no father or mother, you know, perhaps he has a woman there too, because he's been alone. But don't you fret, Moran, he'll come back and be a good husband. What's a Hittite woman? A passing shadow.

She did not fret. She was simply impatient to start her life in this place, which she felt more accustomed to each morning. She liked to step outdoors and gaze at the high cliff and at the few trees that looked like grasshoppers against its tall body. She cleaned the house and cleaned it again. She found the copper mirror in the storage space and sat burnishing it for hours. She waited some more.

On the fourth day Salu came home. Moran jumped up awkwardly to greet him, her eyes lowered with embarrassment because she did not have her best dress on and her bridal veil was not unpacked. Perhaps he would not find her pretty. Her feet were much too big.

She ran to paint her eyes, her hands trembling. In her haste she could not find her perfume vial. She ran again to bring Salu a bowl of water for his feet, and back to her bundles to search in vain for the veil.

Salu did not look at her. He washed his feet methodically, eyes blinking hard. He glanced up furtively only once, when she brought him the food she had made.

It smelled good and they ate with quiet hunger. He asked about her journey. She would have liked to tell him about the whirlstorm, but did not know how. They ate side by side, fumbling for words.

Slowly, the words came. There were not many of them and they were not very big. Now, however, when they looked at each other, their glances met and remained there. He saw that she had pretty eyes and felt ashamed of his own that would not stay straight. Blinking, he smiled down at the ground. Moran did not care about his eyes. She liked the way he looked. The silence grew easier.

Toward morning she put her palms on his face. They were tender.

Afterward Salu returned to the Hittites.

They were his friends. The blinkard, they called him. As if his twitch had made him tribeless, they had long ago stopped thinking of him as a Hebrew. Years of eating and drinking their food and sitting up with them nights near the fort had taught him to speak their language like one of them. They were but a few families who had come south to trade with the caravans for copper and alabaster, protected by the Egyptian garrison. They laughed a lot, like people who had seen much. He liked that.

The Egyptians were seldom seen. Sometimes the figure of a soldier or slave flitted by outside, on its way to saddle a horse or make water in the bushes. Sometimes a soldier from the look-out tower shouted an order and a Hittite hurried over, bowed, and lifted his chin high to hear what was wanted. Only when a caravan arrived and a party of armed soldiers rode out to collect the tax for the great god Pharaoh did the Hittites emerge to swoop down on the travelers. For many days raucous cries of buying and selling reached the fort, until the caravan left and there was silence again. The fort was strong. It made itself felt.

Salu kept returning to them, as if unable to tear himself away.

There was a woman involved. Several years older than he, she was as small and thin as a girl, unable to conceive.

She bit her lips and groaned from the heat as she was made by the Hittite women to squat over steaming bowls of scabwort in the hope of unsealing her womb. They unfastened all things in her house, opened every bundle, undid the flaps, unknotted all the ropes and laces. They even let down their hair, and when not a knot or clasp remained and yellow vapors stained the woman's thighs, they called for Salu. Rising from the men's fire to shouts of encouragement, he entered the tent and possessed her quickly, pouring his youthful seed into the thin, dark, scabwort-steamed body. The little squeals she let out were like those caused by the vapors. The other women mimicked them, laughing.

But she did not conceive. She would rather be dead than childless, she said, reaching out her thin arms to Salu. He was her only comfort in the whole desert. He did not know how to appease her.

This time, they knew when he came that there was a woman in his house. The shepherds had told them. The shepherds knew everything; no secret could be kept from them. The Hittite woman was angry. So you have a bride from the mountains, she said. I suppose this is the last your friends will see of you. She had no one else in this place. What would she do without him? She might as well die.

He did his best to console her. He would still come to see her, he said. And he had at home two gold anklets and a copper mirror that had been his mother's. He would bring them to her, too.

He knew he would not. He turned to go dejectedly, covering his retreat with promises.

Ever since Moran's arrival, Salu was a torn man. In the Hittite camp, he longed for home. At home, he missed the Hittites.

Once Moran showed him the mirror she had burnished. Furious, he turned away from her. When you sleep your lids are quiet, Salu, she said softly. He refused to talk to her and she tried making herself small while he sulked. Sometimes, when his whole face twitched, she laid her palms on his eyelids. They beat against her like a wiry cricket and then grew calm again.

Sometimes he yielded. Sometimes he fled. He was short-tempered, like a man who owes an inhumanly large debt that can never be paid. Each time he left in the morning, she gathered his hairs from the woolen tufts of the pallet and wove them into her own.

T here was little rain that year. The winter brought much lightning, flashing silently and quickly in the sky. They stared at it uneasily, thinking each time that perhaps now the rains would come. But the sky was niggardly. At most it released a few drops, not enough to quench a man's thirst. The moistened earth gave off a strong, questing smell as if rutting for water. The planted seeds stirred and fell still again. The roots of the bushes dug deeper, groped in the darkness, and gave up. What little rain there was soon was over. One could feel the roots aching in the ground.

Each morning a villager descended worriedly to the plain and kicked at the sand to check for moisture. But the sand was dry and crumbly and there was nothing to make its grains stick. Only in the bottomland could a few sprouts of grass be seen. Wherever a camel had trod in autumn, leaving its hollow print, little tired smudges of green stretched to the horizon. It was barely enough to sustain the herds. Life breathed shallowly.

They felt wasted and bitter. They knew that God had broken his promise. The land was bad; it had not yielded to them. Vipers and scorpions sprouted from its rocks, watered by the villagers' sweat—yes, they had sweated mightily and had nothing to show for it but a bit of barley. Where, they grumbled, was the father who spoke to Moses at Sinai, tricking the people like children to follow Moses and Joshua? They were more dead than alive in this place. And Joshua had vanished too. One by one the years passed and he was not heard from. Suppose he was dead; to whom could they take their complaints? Perhaps there is no God at all in this place, they muttered. Perhaps he stayed in the mountains. There he sits with the priests in the tabernacle, the smell of sacrifice in his nostrils. He lacks nothing and we are abandoned, no longer his sons.

The elders hushed them and they fell silent for a while, but the murmurings did not cease.

At night they fell asleep languidly, exhausted by solitude. In the morning they rose without knowing what for.

Moran paid no heed to any of this. She was with child and carried it well, going swiftly from chore to chore and singing as she walked and worked. Tall and sure of herself, she strode through the village on the flat soles of her feet as though in an air of her own. Sometimes, longing to talk with her sisters in the mountains, to chat and laugh with them, her heart grew heavy at the thought of the distance between them that she might never cross again. But then the child would stir within her and make her smile. Lie down, you, she would tell it, your time hasn't come yet. Its tiny, caressing movements overcame all sorrow.

She could no longer remember her old life. Issachar's home had faded into a mirage. Around her was vast, empty space, three thorn trees clustered over here, five more, far away, over there. The broad, simple days, the endless sky, the humble hills: all were hers. Each time she passed, Hofra the midwife looked at her and said: You will have a good birth, my child.

One morning, while she was gathering sorrel in the hills, a heavy blow struck her belly. A stone, she thought in alarm. Someone has thrown a stone at me.

The second stone struck her too. She covered her belly with both hands and looked around in bafflement until she saw a skinny woman hiding in a clump of bushes. She knew it must be the Hittite.

Moran doubled over and headed quickly back toward the village, protecting her stomach. The Hittite woman followed close behind, dodging from bush to bush and thorn tree to thorn tree while throwing whatever she laid hands on: stones, branches, dirt, dry roots. Lungs bursting, Moran ran as fast as she could. For a moment the missiles stopped and she thought the Hittite woman was gone. A moment later the heaviest stone of all, the hard essence of the woman's hate, struck the hand shielding her belly. The Hittite woman stood openly facing Moran a while longer, triumphant, then slipped off and disappeared.

She flung herself on her bed, panting jerkily. She kept her hands on her stomach, ignoring her bloody fingers. She could not feel the child move.

She stared at the ceiling, stricken by fear, not knowing if it was day or night. Her mouth was dry. She was afraid to make a sound or move a limb until the evil had passed from her and the child.

The sun sank low in the west. From the doorway she heard Salu talking with the shepherd boy. The child stirred within her, weakly at first, then more and more.

She rose and went to make supper.

She did not tell Salu. It was as if telling might reawaken the evil of it. When he asked about the red bruise on her hand, she said she had slipped on a rock. For several days she went about with a dagger, though she knew that in her state she was no match for the Hittite woman. The prisoner of her pregnancy, she squeezed the knife handle with pent-up anger. She felt naked, bared to every ill wind, powerless to defend herself and her child.

For a while she suspected every bush and rut in the path. But the Hittite woman did not come again.

Τhe winter was very cold. Fierce winds blew from the desert, piercing clothes and cracks in the walls. The days had no light. The gray ridge line faded into a gray sky, beneath which pallid souls lay sick in bed, heavy with affliction. Even the healthy wrapped themselves in their cloaks and rarely ventured outside.

The flocks stayed close to the houses. They nibbled what they could and returned to huddle together. The shepherds were afraid of nomads and hugged the village too. For days they all waited. They knew that if there was rain they would live, and that if none came some of them would not see the next summer.

The young ones complained the most. At first in whispers and then with growing courage, half a dozen of them declared that God was far away, no one could say what he wanted, and since they had no prophet, God had to be found and brought back. They would look for him high and low until he agreed to be the father he was at Sinai.

At first the villagers shrugged. How was such a thing to be done? Was God to be bound with thick rope and dragged back to the desert by force? He would come or not as he pleased. And as for Moses, who had brought them to this land, no one even knew where he was buried. There was not so much as a grave by which to pray.

The days passed without rain. Vipers and scorpions invaded the huts, slithering in the corners. There were too many of them to kill. Not even incense drove them away. Coughs, rasps, and the cries of children came from everywhere.

One night, when the wind was so wild that no one dared step outside, someone remembered that there was a Levite among them, a man named Yekuel, the son of a daughter of the tribe of Levi.

Perhaps he knew what God wanted.

They went to Yekuel. He was a morose, quick-spoken man of about forty. Perhaps they should offer a sacrifice, he said. God liked a sacrifice and might countenance them if given one. He could not be sure of it, though, because at Sinai their fathers had made no offerings, and yet God was with them there, at their side day and night.

They interrupted him impatiently. Why was he beating around the bush? Sinai was Sinai. This was a different land beneath a different sky, and all who dwelt in it sacrificed to their gods. A land of offerings it was, and they must offer the best that they had so that God might savor its sweet scent and be appeased.

Yekuel wavered for a day or two and consented.

A commotion gripped the village. Sheep and goats were prepared, good clothes were taken out and scrubbed as clean as possible: lo, soon it would come to pass, God would be with them again as with their fathers. Were they not his children who sought to please him? He would return their gift sevenfold.

The wind died down a bit. A good omen, it was said.

At midday they gathered at the foot of the highest hill. Family by family they assembled, each with a bleating sheep or goat held by a boy. Yekuel stood in a tall turban on the hilltop, surrounded by young men with knives. He had been there all morning, chanting a long prayer whose words no one could make out.

One by one the boys climbed the hill to present the animals' throats to the sharp-edged knives. The sheep baaed with a hideous fear. Seized by the terror of death, a few broke away and fled; run down quickly, they were pinned pitilessly in the harsh vise of their captors' legs and kicked and dragged back to the killing grounds. Their tremulous bleats came from everywhere, from hilltop and bottomland, as if from the scared earth itself. Yekuel went on petitioning the heavens for mercy.

Sheep and goats were slaughtered one after another, their blood soaking the sand with red stains that soon turned to puddles. Boys inserted sticks beneath the hides and blew to help loosen them from the flesh. A few of the animals were still alive and writhed as they were skinned. Now and then Yekuel's voice, like a breaking wave of supplication loudly assented to by all, rose above the din. The pile of dead animals kept growing. Stiff legs sticking out of the heap, they were bright red and gaunt-looking without their skin. Children capered up and down the hill, roused by the smell of blood, their cries mingling with the waves of prayer and the terrified bleats.

The winter day was soon over, passing unnoticed from dull, gray light to darkness. They could feel their hunger now, made ravenous by the mound of carcasses and the blood-scented air.

Yet when they went to ask for their meat—let each man roast his share and feed his house—Yekuel refused. The sacrifice, he said, was God's. Cursed be the man who ate from it. Was it to rob their own father that they wished?

But there was no stopping them. Snatching skinned sheep, a few flushed men hurried home to start fires. Three or four others bestrode the pile, throwing sides of meat to outstretched arms. Still others rent their clothes and shouted that it was a sin; the sacrifice was being despoiled, the whole village would die for it. Men fought over the meat, yelling as they tore it from one another's hands. Blood flowed from a man's struck nose onto the carcass in his hands.

No one knew who lit the huge bonfire at the foot of the hill. Suddenly it was there, huge and billowing smoke. The quickest hurried to throw their meat into it, the smell of the sizzling, dripping fat making their senses swoon. They ate with jaws snapping at muscle and bone, sucking the red, half-raw marrow, famished for food and for the fullness that never came; perhaps this time, just once, they will be sated.

Afterwards a large circle formed. Despite his anger, Yekuel left his corner and joined it, a turbaned giant by the light of the fire. Young and old, the villagers called upon the names of God, every male in the village stamping out the dance. Merciful One, they chanted as if possessed, Mighty One, Powerful One, Compassionate One. On and on.

Moran gazed at the circle of flickering light, unable to move. Now and then she caught sight of Salu silhouetted against the fire, stamping and moaning in the frenzy of the dance before whirling away again. The women sat outside the circle, watching. One brought a pair of cymbals and struck it rhythmically, but the sound was drowned out.

They watched for a while and went home. The whirling men did not notice that they were gone.

Moran was near the village when she felt the first labor pains. Seeking a quiet place to give birth in, far from the revels, she went to Hofra's and called out to her from the doorway. But Hofra hugged her when she emerged and said: Come, my daughter, I'll take you home, that's where a child should be born if it's not to be a wanderer all its life.

She leaned on Hofra, the pains coming more often as they walked. The midwife lit the lamp and tied a harness to a pole in the doorway to serve as a brace. Then she made a place for Moran to squat, talking all the time, as if to fill the room with words that left not a crack for fear or evil. But Moran was not afraid. She listened carefully to her contractions and pulled at the harness when they grew strong. Hofra held her from behind. Push, my child, push, she said, you're almost there. And Moran, hurrying to get there, gripped the midwife's arms and gave birth as if a tide had surged far out of her, never to return.

It's a boy, said Hofra, holding the infant high. When he failed to cry, she said that he must have been frightened in the womb. Over and over she slapped his back until he gurgled and made a sound—at first a faint one, then stronger. Moran held him tightly. Hofra cleaned up, still talking all the while. She did not bother to go tell the men. The dancing circle was far off, echoing through the desert like a beating heart.

Salu came home before dawn, hair and clothes smelling strongly of smoke. He briefly froze when he saw the child; then he did a little jig as if still dancing. He would make a great banquet in the boy's honor, he said, the whole village would be invited. He swayed back and forth, ashen in the dawn light. Weary, he fell asleep.

Moran moved away from the smell.

For a while the sheepskins lay on the hill, gnawed on or dragged away at night by the beasts of the desert. A thick, black fur of buzzing flies squirmed on them revoltingly during the day. The stench carried far. Finally the skins vanished, the last of them gone by evening. Yet the clouds of flies still hovered, searching for what was no longer there. They circled, found nothing, and settled on the villagers' eyes.

Two days later the wind picked up. At first the clouds came like a host of busy men with no time, released a probe of rain here and there, and moved on. Then they merged to form a thick cover in the west. Crows wheeled beneath it, as if trapped beneath its weight. Once more the sky burned with silent lightning at night, flaring and dying in a heavenly dumb show. The villagers stood in their doorways, staring at the strange sky that lit up the plain, the hills, and the chalky rise in sharp flashes. They talked in whispers, chilled and awed to the bone.

They awoke in the morning to the sound of rain. For three days it poured without stop. Then it was over. From the gully came a thunderous rumble, announcing a flood. They ran to see it, barefoot and shouting at each other, and arrived just in time to watch it go by, a wall of turbid brown water rushing down the creek and sweeping away the banks as it burst through every barrier. For several days a film of water covered everything. Then it sank into the ground.

They had had no chance to trap it. Still, it was better than nothing. Yekuel went about like a king in his turban. The villagers grabbed at the folds of his cloak, thankful, ever so thankful. All agreed that the sacrifice had gone well. Next year they would offer it again. And this time they would not eat of it; no, absolutely not. They knew now that it was a sin.

For all their talk, however, they knew that the rain was not enough. The flood had slipped through their hands. When the sun came out and the dry winds blew, the moisture would quickly vanish. Blessing had eluded them again. Their voices were hollow when they spoke of it.

Although now and then dancers formed new circles, their hearts were no longer in it. A month went by. A glance at the flocks was enough to tell them that there would be no more sacrifices that year. The sheep were with young, the lambs were not yet grown. Perhaps when summer came. They stared at the ground, avoiding Yekuel's eyes.

The Hittite woman would not give up. Each time Salu came, she clutched desperately at the threads of his life as if at a garment she could pull him by. She was an empty woman, she said. For years, day in and day out, he had eaten her meat and drunk her water, and now it meant nothing to him. Why didn't he take a knife and kill her? He had already done it in his heart.

He held his head, not knowing what to answer.

One morning Salu took his son and brought him to the Hittite woman. When Moran came home from milking, the child was gone.

Salu returned at midday. He spoke quickly, feverishly. You'll have many more sons, Moran. And daughters. And she is barren, she has no child. God will be good to us because of it. Your womb will be full. The house will be noisy with children. How can you deny her even one child?

Moran collapsed on the ground, crying for justice, justice, until he thought his head would split. Driven wild by her cries, he shouted that he did not know what justice was, or where it could be found, or who owned it. She could go look for it herself, he yelled, running from the house.

He did not come home that night. He did not go to the

Hittite camp, either. He lay wrapped in his cloak on the ground, unrepentant. I should have listened to the elders and trod on her foot when I wed her, he thought. That's why she won't listen to me. He tossed back and forth. Sleep did not come.

Neighbor women came and helped Moran to her feet. Wiping her face, they spoke gently. What can you do, they asked with ancient, habituated sorrow. Whom can you turn to? He is your master and will do what he wants. There were tears in their eyes. That evening, slinking and shamefaced, one of them slipped back into the house and returned the embroidery stolen on the day of Moran's arrival in the village. Here, Moran, she said in a whisper, it's yours. I am not a thieving woman. I just couldn't resist the red. And all the green. This village is so dreary.

Moran neither saw nor heard. At times she thought she heard the child breathing as he awoke; any second he would begin to cry. But when she ran to look for him she found only high, cold silence that left her staring uncomprehendingly at her empty hands.

In the middle of the night she reached for the dagger and made up her mind to go to the Hittite camp and bring the child back by force. Let whoever wanted join her; if not, she would go alone. She would murder the Hittite.

And yet suppose, she thought suddenly, the fear rushing into her eyes, that the child were killed in the scuffle? He was so tiny. She sat down heavily, struck dumb by anger and fear, her hands groping blindly for the warm little body. The child must be hungry. Who was nursing him now? Milk flowed in abundance from her breasts, wetting the bodice of her dress. She shivered.

The next day Salu brought the child back. Sullen and embarrassed, he entered the house with the bitterly crying baby in his arms. The father of the Hittite woman had told him to return the boy. The Hittites were afraid. The blinkard will only get us into trouble, they had said with narrowed eyes. His brothers and uncles will come for the child and thrash us. Snatching it from the Hittite woman, they practically threw it at Salu, as if it were a bundle of poison. Here, let him take it and go.

Moran looked at the child. It was wearing strange clothes and smelled strangely. She clutched it, uncertain if it was really hers, the fruit of her womb. It cried more strongly as it felt her presence, and she unthinkingly put her nipple in its mouth. The milk came, and then the tears.

His eyes downcast, Salu laid a cautious hand on the boy's head. He felt empty. Moran shrank back from him. Each time he touched the child, or even looked at it, her fury returned.

He said nothing. His touch was soft. Apart from that nothing was left of him, not even words. Sometimes he wiped the tears roughly from his eyes.

In the days that followed, something wary and tentative seemed to open in him. He quickened his pace as he neared home, eager to glimpse the child as if for the first time. Yet when Moran turned it protectively away from him each time he appeared, he noticed and hung his head. Once, guilt-ridden, he said to her: I'm not a bad man, Moran. She didn't answer.

Her body slumped in on itself. She went about her chores with curt, locked movements and did not talk to Salu or even look at him. And he, as if having lost his sense of direction, never even glanced at the Hittite camp. Entrenched in their grievances, they used fewer and fewer words.

Slowly they came to terms with their new, silent life. There was much to do that year. Hiram and his sons had brought grape vines from the mountains, and the whole village was busy piling stone mounds around them. Visible from afar, the mounds spread over the sand like dark landmarks. Moran spent whole days planting, her baby close by in the shade, digging irrigation holes, firming the earth at the vines' base, covering it with stones to absorb what dew there was. She felt she had to answer with her whole being for each leaf. Who else would look after it? She carried water from far off. The vines took. In no time the hillside was full of them.

Salu, too, plunged into his work as into a pool of water. The villagers had begun hewing and plastering large cisterns and cutting channels to them in the rocks. It started with two or three men and soon spread to the others. At times the amount of work daunted them. The sun beat down. Their aching hands were chapped and cracked. But they persisted, and by the next winter, water was flowing down smooth conduits. They stood quietly gazing at the still barely filling cisterns, their weary arms folded on their chests with the hands tucked under them. Soon, soon the hillside would be crisscrossed with channels and the last of the plaster slapped on. The flood would not escape again. They would catch it like a leopard in a trap.

Moran gave birth every year, first to another son, and then to a daughter, and then to a son again, all conceived in silence. Her births were easy. Hofra wrapped herself in a shawl, took her midwife's bundle, and hurried over. Your children are quick, my daughter, she chuckled on the way, if you don't hold onto them a bit longer, their souls won't catch up with their bodies, and then where will we be? But they entered the world as if they had always been in it. Moran kept her clenched hands on her dress as the women showed Salu the new baby, the old fear returning with each birth. The silence between them was beyond breaking. The speech had as though deserted their bodies. Sometimes Salu cried at night. He did it quietly, so as not to wake her, and fell asleep again.

One day a Hittite boy came looking for Salu. Salu saw him from afar, running quickly over the plain, a small figure waving its arms. There's news, Salu, he shouted from afar, news, the soldiers have left the fort and gone back to Egypt, Pharaoh recalled them, the fort has been empty for two days, it's empty, no one is in it, Salu.

Salu caught his breath and began to walk slowly back to the village, wiping stone dust from his hands. Then his pace quickened to a run. Hoarsely he called for the villagers. A few flushed-looking men gathered round him, shouting in all directions that the fort was empty. God had delivered it to them. The Egyptians were gone.

The glad tidings spread like wildfire. Men came running from the waterworks, from the pasture, from the dam, surrounding Salu. He knew the fort. They would follow him. It was empty, empty.

Not everyone joined. Hiram listened and went angrily home to tell his two sons to stay out of it. But he did not insist very hard; he knew they would not obey him. Pretending not to hear, they ran off. Three or four other men stood shrugging for a minute and then went back to their work. Our chores are near and the fort is far, they said, all the screamers will be back empty-handed before sundown.

The wildfire seized all the rest.

Like a flash flood they raced across the plain, brandishing bars and knives, stumbling and righting themselves, clambering up the cliff, panting in single file along a narrow terrace, clutching at each other as they dashed down a steep ravine spraying dust, and scratched by thorn bushes. Soon, soon they would reach the pool. There would be plenty of water.

The fort cast its shadow before them. Several Hittites stood there expectantly, with obsequious laughs, as if they had known all along. One made a sweeping bow and pointed to the fort as if inviting important guests. The Hittites did not approach Salu or talk with him. Nor did he look at them. They stood with slit eyes, half-fawning and half-mocking, waiting to see what the conquerors would do.

Overjoyed, the villagers breached the gate and swept through the entranceway into the narrow, dark corridors, their running feet echoing in the lower and upper chambers. The huge shadow devoured them, ancient and smelling of stone.

The fort was not empty. Down below, in the stables, two slaves had been left behind. Horror rising in their eyes, they tried protecting their heads with their hands. The villagers butchered them quickly.

One of the upper rooms was locked. They passed it by and only broke into it the next day. A slave lay wallowing on sacks of foodstuffs, unable to rise, his stomach stretched to the bursting point. Hearing the invaders, he had begun to eat all he could to keep it out of their hands: dates and beans and flour and bread and chick-peas and honey. The food was Pharaoh's; no stranger must touch it. He ate and ate. His vomit was everywhere. He would have eaten the sacking too, had he been able.

They stood over him laughing. He laughed wretchedly back, as if it were some kind of a joke. Half-digested food and offal spilled out with the guts when he was pierced, fouling the room and its vicinity. They left him lying on the sacks, guarding them even in death.

Someone went to get the Hittites to clean up. But they were gone. Their little camp looked barred to the world.

They ran to the pool. A deep ravine, walled by flat slabs of white rock, led down to it. The shrill call of a single bird that flew away was all that broke the silence. An outcrop of rock hung over the pool like a gateway. There was a smell of still water. Here and there, like thin locks of hair, saltbush grew from the white walls.

They leaped into the water, drinking it, pouring it over heads and beards, washing hands and faces with it. But the water was not fresh. It was brackish and salty. Afterwards their skins smarted in the sun.

Salu wandered through the empty fort, running his hands over its stones and peering into its rooms and niches with their remnants of a former life. A strip of leather. Bits of a clay scarab. Some marred parchment. The rusted handle of a tool. The dimness was stony and deep. He walked on, stooping in the low passageways, touching the large, strong stones again and again. He did not know what he was looking for. Once he said in a low voice, You are a slippery she-goat, mother, and laughed briefly. He knew his mother was not in the fort and never had been.

But it captivated him. This was a strong place, he thought, with a commander and a god to bow to. A place well-protected.

From day to day the fort fitted him more, like a second skin. In the dim light he hardly blinked. He liked the deep echoes and dim tunnels with their thick, darkness-doubled walls. Sometimes, at sundown, he climbed to the roof and gazed into the distance as far as the High Negev and the great Salt Rift, pride swelling in him like newborn strength. Why, the twenty-second year of his life had not yet passed and the fort was his. Everyone hung on his words, for it was he who had brought them here.

Yekuel found him in an upper room. He stepped solemnly up to him and said, speaking slowly as if bestowing his words: You are king of the fort, Salu. Give a thanks-offering and remember that it was God who guided you.

Salu was taken aback. Being a king was beyond his ken. So was giving thanks. He was glad when Yekuel left him alone again.

At first they transported the water from the pool on donkeys, waterskins sloshing, the children welcoming them merrily as they went back and forth a few times a day. The water was poured onto crops and into cisterns with a gurgle they had not heard for a long time. Stains of moisture, little round stamps of blessing, appeared around the trees even in the heat of day. It was a sight they could not get their fill of.

But the trail was hard on the donkeys, who balked, over-heated, at the cliff. The salty water did not taste good either. They went for it less and less as the heat grew worse.

A few women and children plucked up the courage to join their menfolk in the fort. The children splashed happily in the water. But before the drop of night they hurried back to the village, as if returning to overstepped bounds. They feared spending the night in the fort. It remained a strange place.

Moran never went there. If her master wished, she said, he could visit her at home. She had four small children. The trip was too much for her.

Salu did not press her. Sometimes he came back for a day or two, quickly patting the heads of the children who sprang to greet him. At night he and Moran held tight to each other as if they alone were left in the world. In the morning they went their separate ways without a glance.

He would hasten back to the fort. It was not to be with the Hittites, as Moran thought. They had withdrawn into a world of their own, and Salu had stopped thinking about the Hittite woman after the episode with his son. What did he care about the Hittites? They were a shiftless lot. Sometimes he told himself: I am king of the fort. Perhaps he would take a concubine or two. What man would deny him his daughters? Not even Yekuel, if only he wanted them.

But he knew he would do no such thing. Moran was in his bones.

The summer was short. Autumn winds blew early down the great plain, sweeping sand, fluff, and tumbleweed before them, flattening the smoke from the cooking fires in the yards and scattering the ashes. Smoke blew into the houses and made their inhabitants rub their stinging eyes. Here and there a few drops of rain fell, glittering on the rock-face. A donkey or two was still driven to the pool. Mostly, they waited.

In the middle of the night, beneath a late, slender moon, with a loud clatter of hoof beats on the rock, the Egyptians returned to the fort. Like lightning they came, easily breaking through the gate, racing through the rooms with drawn swords as if goaded by the smell of fear.

The killing was swift. Hofra's husband, Honi, and his two sons died in their bedding, hair disheveled from sleep and eyes bulging. Three other men were found in the upper rooms and the stables. The fort echoed with the sounds of running steps, sudden thrusts, and hoarse grunts in the darkness.

Salu dodged between the legs of the first soldier to enter the room in the wan moonlight, bowled over the man behind him, snatched his sword, and stood facing them. As if he could, must, floor them with his voice, the only thing he still possessed, tearing a hole with it in the nightmare, he let out a terrible, sobbing roar.

Ten more soldiers burst into the now crowded room. They shoved Salu outside disdainfully, sticking him with swords and left him by the staircase baffled why the life was ebbing out of him. Hiram, he said reproachfully, why don't you do something. His large hands slapped the floor once and again, and he was dead.

The soldiers proceeded to the Hittite camp. You betrayed us, they charged. In vain the Hittites pleaded, swearing that they had not helped the Hebrews, that their camp had been barred all along. The soldiers ignored them. They killed the men, looted what they could, and trotted the bawling flock of women to the fort. Dark blood mingled with mud and smashed utensils.

The fort went back to its old ways.

Moran was left alone. For years she went on fighting with Salu in her dreams, shouting as loud as she could until her anger melted away in hot, sorrowful tears. She would awake and sit up, unkempt and bewildered, as weary as after a long day's work, her arms and legs spread out in search of Salu's body. Why weren't his arms around her? But there was nothing there. She hungered for him as in the first days of their marriage, as if death had turned around and become a new beginning. Soon, soon he would come for her to lay her hands on his eyes as then, when she still had been tender. Once she dreamed that she was on her way to bring him back. She walked and walked on a long, tiring road and found him sitting alone in the desert beneath a blazing sun. He was a boy of about twelve and his hands were lilies. With a bright look he told her that he could not return with her, for his father had sought to kill him.

She was with him all night, from the time she lay down until the time she rose. Her dreams woke her frightened children. She hugged them tightly, her face wet. The house grew deep.

The old, impassable distance between village and fort was back again. They never looked in its direction. Consumed by defeat, stricken by mourning, they sat hurting listlessly until the udders of the flocks were full and had to be milked. Wiping their tears, they shuffled to the animals. Instead of giving them his blessing, God had toyed with them. He had given and taken as always, but he took far more than he gave. No one was prepared to listen when Yekuel said that God was wroth because of their sins. Go put on your turban, Yekuel, they mocked bitterly, we are not children. God had toyed with them enough. No more.

The village grew greatly. New houses closed the gaps between the first tumbledown huts and climbed up the hillside to the view of the Wilderness of Zin. By the great dam, nine years in the making, sat launderers, wash spread in the sun. From the cisterns came the clap of buckets against the walls and lower chambers. The trees were strong.

Across the dry gully, where a levee now straddled the grounds where they had danced themselves senseless, a market sprang up. At first no more than a mat or two for the wares, then more and more. Wandering shepherds came from afar, stragglers in tattered clothes. They looked on dumbly for a while before making a place for themselves with a mat and a balance scale. The villagers suffered them until they built on one of the hilltops a high altar for the Ashera, which was angrily torn down. The shepherds put up no resistance. They knew that their gods were weak and that the god of the Hebrews was stronger. Not as strong as Pharaoh, though.

One day Hiram came to visit Moran. He was a very old man

with a broad, heavy belly carried in front of him like a table. Happy to see him, she did her hair and radiantly set out bread, olive oil, and wine.

She thought he had come to propose a match with one of his sons. But it turned out that he wanted her for himself. With a look of compassion, he said, You are tired, my daughter. Once your feet chattered when you walked and now they stammer. Come, rest in my house.

He was not angry when she declined. All he asked was to be allowed to visit now and then, to chat a bit and drink the wine of her good vines. In the entire village, no vines were as good as Moran's.

His blessing when he rose to go was that God should always be with her; and she, the old sorrow back in her face, begged his forgiveness in a whisper. She was not worth Father Hiram's anger, but she would rather God stayed away from her. Let him ignore her in his heaven, because the gods burned all when they came. They brought death and sickness and madness and drought. It's all we can do to make good what they ruin. Spare us both their honey and their sting. We're no match for them.

Astonished, he did not know what to say.

Still, he laid his hands on her head in leaving. They were old hands, with skin that no longer clove to the flesh. For a long time he stood blessing her and her sons while she bowed her head without objection. Her eyes were moist.

One summer the musicians came. They rode into the village on donkeys loaded with instruments, looking about them to gauge whether this was a place they could earn some bread in.

That night, when the market was empty, they sat down in it and played. The whole village turned out to hear them. No one went to sleep. Their melodies were sweet, brought from the mountains, from a time of figs, carobs, pomegranates, and olives, of birdsong, golden light, and the scent of cassia, from the lost maze of childhood before they had set out for this place. For many days they did not let the musicians leave. They should stay a little longer, just a little longer. The villagers brought them food and gifts. They had not known how thirsty they were.

They asked the musicians questions. About Ma'aleh Hoglah. The musicians shrugged. It was a small and poor place, they said. Most of its inhabitants had left because of the Canaanites. One was lucky to find a house that had two goats and a donkey or wasn't in a state of collapse. This village was ten times bigger.

They listened, baffled.

Then they asked if there was a king in Israel. Or a prophet. No, said the musicians, there was neither. But there was a judge; the people had chosen him. Ben-Anat was his name. Could the villagers never have heard of him? Everyone knew his name.

They were abashed. Perhaps, they said, the time had come to visit their brothers in the mountains. Too long had they walked after sheep dung in the desert. Years had come and years had gone, and they knew nothing of the world.

Moran brought the musicians food and drink at night. Beside herself, she sat listening to their songs. Once she asked one of the playing boys about her sisters, the daughters of Issachar. He had never heard of them. Many of the girls from Ma'aleh Hoglah are Canaanite bondwomen, he said. Perhaps your sisters are too. The place has not done well.

She hung her head.

That night, while her sons were asleep, he came and stayed until morning.

Whenever the musicians returned in the years to come, he came to Moran just as gently. She took him in, never knowing where he began and the melody ended, whether she was home in the desert or in Ma'aleh Hoglah.

Then the musicians stopped coming.

$\mathbf{M}$oran sat on a rock, looking out at the cliffs. All morning she had been gathering fennel to brew balm for a grandson, and she was tired. Her sons were now older than Salu when he died. How strange that was, boys older than their father. It took someone wiser than herself to understand it. She sat down to rest, slipping the shoes from her large feet and turning to face the wind that blew from the white hills of Zin.

Wind, she said smiling, you are like a man, you start with small caresses, and then what am I to do?

She sat, her hands in her lap, the warm air stroking her face as if the whole strong wilderness were breathing close to her, quiet and warm.

And when the wind grew very strong, she shut her eyes.